CAMP ROLLING HILLS

SMELLY

SLIMEY

Stacy Davidowitz

Amulet Books
New York

Library of Congress Cataloging-in-Publication Data

Names: Davidowitz, Stacy, author.
Title: Camp Rolling Hills / by Stacy Davidowitz.
Description: New York : Amulet Books, [2016] | Series: Camp Rolling Hills ; Book 1 | Summary: "Stephanie (a.k.a. 'Slimey') and Bobby (a.k.a. 'Smelly') have concerns regarding their families back home. Stephanie is returning to the camp she adores; Bobby is a first-time camper who does not really understand lots of what is going on around him during his first exposure to life at summer camp"— Provided by publisher.
Identifiers: LCCN 2015022812 | ISBN 9781419718854 (paperback)
Subjects: | CYAC: Camps—Fiction. | Humorous stories. | BISAC: JUVENILE FICTION / Humorous Stories. | JUVENILE FICTION / Social Issues / Friendship. | JUVENILE FICTION / Love & Romance.
Classification: LCC PZ7.1.D3365 Fi 2016 | DDC [Fic]—dc23
LC record available at http://lccn.loc.gov/2015022812

Printed and bound in U.S.A.
10 9 8 7 6 5 4 3 2 1

Amulet Books are available at special discounts when purchased in quantity for premiums and promotions as well as fundraising or educational use. Special editions can also be created to specification. For details, contact specialsales@abramsbooks.com or the address below.

ABRAMS
THE ART OF BOOKS SINCE 1949
115 West 18th Street
New York, NY 10011
www.abramsbooks.com

For the fam and our one-day Davidowitz Camp

Are We There Yet?!

Fourteen, fifteen, sixteen, seventeen! Slimey counted the rows from the front of the bumpy, AC-deprived bus to where she stood almost three-quarters back. It was the right row for her to be in, she decided, because it was her fourth summer at the Hills, and she wasn't the oldest camper but definitely not the youngest, either.

"Hey! Take a seat back there!"

Slimey didn't think the bus driver was shouting specifically at her—other kids were standing, too—but she thought she'd better sit down, just in case. It wasn't like she had anyone to talk to in another row—she was just afraid she'd explode if she didn't stretch her legs. She was shaking, she was so excited.

"I *will* pull over. Don't make me say it again!"

She could understand if one of the newbie One Tree Hill girls was still standing, but the Notting Hill girls, now scurrying into their seats, should know better, since they were going into ninth grade. Upper Campers should be good role models, after all.

"Thank you!" the bus driver called in a raspy voice. Slimey

guessed it was from shouting all the time. That or smoking. Shouting, she hoped, since smoking was bad for you.

Slimey gave a silent sigh and leaned against the window for some shut-eye. Two hours had passed already, and if she napped for just an hour more, she'd wake up at camp! That plan lasted all of three heartbeats before she got antsy. *List-making time!* She reached into her frayed purple L.L.Bean backpack— it was three years old, but it was perfect for camp, because she could get it dirty and not care—and took out her sketchbook. She got to work.

Things to Do Now That I'm in Anita Hill Cabin
(Upper Camp!)

1. Be a good role model.

2. Make a special camp collage of my friends and our inside jokes.

3. Box-stitch extra lanyard key chains for Mom, since stress makes her lose her keys.

4. Spend A LOT of time with my camp sister/soul sister/BFF.

Slimey had always wanted a sister, and she treasured the times she and Melman pretended they were fraternal twins separated at birth. Fraternal, because they looked nothing alike. Twins, because their birthdays were only three days apart, and they'd always understood exactly how the other felt.

Until last summer. But that wasn't Melman's fault. Slimey couldn't expect anyone to understand that kind of throat-closing, belly-plummeting pain. She didn't want anyone to, either.

She'd gotten used to the *I feel bad for you* smiles and awkward pats on the back. They didn't make her feel like curling up in a ball under fifty fleece blankets anymore. They just unleashed a few seconds of heartache, like eating Pop Rocks with Sprite. She could deal with that level of pain on her own. She had to. All Slimey wanted was for everything to stay amazing at camp, like it always was before.

She grimaced as she lifted her practically Krazy Glued leg from the green leathery seat. It left a sweat stain, which was embarrassing, so she put it right back where it was. She didn't really care about that stuff—wouldn't care if it was any of her cabinmates sitting next to her—but the actual girl sitting next to her was one of the Notting Hill Cabin campers. The two girls weren't close—they'd never even spoken—and Slimey knew they probably wouldn't talk the whole trip. Unless the Notting Hill girl saw the stain and said, "Ew." But Slimey doubted even that would happen, because Notting Hill was in the aisle seat, talking to her friends. They were two-thirds of the way there, and the Notting Hill girl hadn't even glanced her way, so the chances that their ride would continue in silence were, like, a hundred percent. Maybe ninety-two.

Slimey knelt up on her seat, wishing she'd find a familiar face. More specifically, a face of one of her cabinmates. One she'd covered with kisses or painted a pretty squirrel on or woken up next to every summer since being a One Tree Hiller.

Melman had always been her bus buddy, and Slimey wished she was here now instead of flying from Heathrow to JFK to take the Long Island bus with Missi. She had a hopeful thought, as fleeting as a camera flash, that maybe Jamie had decided to take the Paramus bus instead of going with Jenny like she always did. Slimey knelt higher to triple-check, but Jamie wasn't on the bus—no surprise there. Slimey knew better than to think the J-squad could separate, even if just for the three-hour trip to Camp Rolling Hills.

Slimey remembered the bus driver's warning and her own promise to be a good role model. If there was a silver lining to what had happened last summer, it was that she'd gotten practice at being one. She had to be strong for her mom. She pictured her dad giving his famous *I'm proud of you* wink, and she shrunk down in her seat, pulling her sticky shins out from beneath her. The suction made a fart noise, which would've made Melman crack up. Notting Hill didn't seem to notice.

Slimey looked out the window as they passed a farm with cows, some milling about, some just standing around, taking it easy. Sometimes she wished she lived on a big open farm instead of in a cramped house in New Jersey, where there was only room for her, her mom, her cockatiel named Lois Lane, and maybe a cat or two if her mom wasn't allergic. Missi had seven cats, not because she lived on a farm, but because her grandparents were hoarders.

Farms made Slimey happy. It meant she was closer to camp than to home.

She flipped to the next page of her sketchbook, but it was already taken up by a drawing of her pink Chuck Taylors. She'd thought she had twenty-eight pages left, but she now figured she was down to twenty-seven, since that page was used up and she'd just made her *Things to Do Now That I'm in Anita Hill Cabin (Upper Camp!)* list.

She opened to the middle of the used pages and flipped through her sketches of Lois 1 and Lois 2, a yellow rose, and a Dustbuster with an eye patch. She'd draw anything, really. Except people. People were really hard, and her sketches never looked like the person. At least, that's what people said when they saw her drawings of them.

Slimey flipped to the very back of the sketchbook, where a worn, folded piece of paper from an old sketchpad was tucked neatly inside. She opened it up on her lap, shook her head, and smiled at the sketch of her Junior Counselor she'd made back when she was a tiny Slimey in One Tree Hill Cabin. Her JC had gotten really mad, because Slimey had made her nose bigger than how she saw it herself. What the JC hadn't understood was that art is interpretive and impressionistic and abstract, and you can't expect someone to draw you exactly like you.

Slimey wished she'd told her JC that before she'd gotten her nose job. It was much smaller and more button-y now. Melman said the operation was for nasal congestion, not vanity, and that Slimey shouldn't feel bad. Their cabinmate Sophie said the JC had gotten her nose bitten off by a vampire, but Sophie was weird and obsessed with vampires and blamed or credited them for pretty much everything.

Slimey began to brainstorm about what she wanted to draw on page twenty-four, but she was sidetracked by the singing, which was really more like on-pitch screaming, coming from the girls behind her.

5

"I live ten months for two.
I come back for you.
I come back for you!!!"

The singing from the older girls in the back made the medium-age girls directly in front of her sing, and then some younger girls all the way up front, and then the boys in the middle, and then the boys in the back, until almost everyone was belting their cabin songs from the summer before. Except for the little new kids way up front, who were either going to be in One Tree Hill Cabin or Bunker Hill Cabin—depending on if they were boys or girls—and had no idea what was happening. Everyone was singing except them and Slimey.

She felt a rush of excitement as her Lauryn Hill Cabin songs from last summer played in her head. She wanted so badly to sing them—her counselor, Sara, had helped her cabinmates write them, and they were amazing, but she knew she couldn't just start singing them by herself. That would be awkward.

She swallowed the melodies and closed her eyes, trying to block out the cacophony of singing and yelling, which she could tell, even without looking, was making the bus driver nuts. She felt a pinch of sorriness for him. But there was nothing for him to say, really—no one was standing anymore, and the songs were silly but appropriate enough by camp-director standards. Plus, the guy had signed up to drive a camp bus, and with camp buses came a lot of noise.

Slimey fumbled with her silver locket—*open, close, open, close. What. Should. I. Draw?* She opened her eyes with anticipation, hoping to see a horse or a sheep or something inspiring, but instead she saw a gas station.

She glanced to her left and noticed that the Notting Hill girl was gone. Likely talking to one of her friends in the back. Or snagging a snack from the sleeping bus counselor. It didn't matter. What she spotted instead was much more interesting.

He was sitting all alone across the aisle. He was about her age, no older than thirteen, no younger than eleven. Even though it must have been a million degrees out, he was wearing a sweatshirt with the hood up. Underneath, he had headphones on. Not earbuds but hard-core headphones, and he was listening to the oldest, biggest iPod she'd ever seen. He was leaning against the window, his knees a little bit bent, the tips of his Nikes against the back of the seat in front of him.

He seemed nervous, and he wasn't singing. To Slimey, that meant one thing and one thing only: he was definitely new.

She thought about saying hey. She knew how he felt, sort of, and she was ready to pull her hair out, not because of all the noise, but because she was simultaneously so bored and excited. Her mouth was about to make the *h* sound, when the bus bumped her forward, sending three of her colored pencils to the floor. She tried to catch them with the bottom of her right Chuck, but they rolled out of foot's reach. As she bent down to get a visual, the blood rushed to the top of her head, making her too dizzy to spot them.

"Hey," a boy's voice called from a few feet away.

Slimey hoisted herself up and stared right into New Boy's warm brown eyes.

"Are you looking for these?" New Boy stretched his arm across the aisle.

She could feel the blood rush back down from the top of her head as she scooted toward him from the window to the aisle on the sticky, leathery seat. She slowly took the colored pencils from his fist. She was trying to make the moment last but was also trying to grab the pencils safely so she didn't get stabbed if there was another big bump. Before she could even say thank you, the Notting Hill girl stood between them, waiting for Slimey to move back to the window seat.

"How many times do I have to say it?" the bus driver yelled. "SIT DOWN!"

Slimey scooted over quickly, and Notting Hill plopped down by her side. She looked at Slimey and smiled, curving her lips open like she was actually going to say something, but then someone called Notting Hill's name, so Notting Hill scooted around onto her knees and faced the back of the bus.

A 100 percent talk-free trip, Slimey thought, smiling to herself. *I was 100 percent right!*

She couldn't really see New Boy through Notting Hill's body—the girl was moving a lot, and the bumpiness of the bus didn't help—but she did see his backpack. L.L.Bean, like hers, but with brown initials threaded in: *R.E.B.* Perfect sketch material.

Slimey was feeling lighter with every mile from home. She kissed her locket, like she did every day, tucked it under her T-shirt, and began to draw.

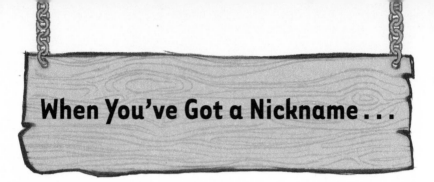

When You've Got a Nickname...

One. More. Hill.

Bobby dragged his wheel-less duffel up the biggest of the four big hills he'd hiked in the last ten minutes. He'd passed soccer fields and volleyball courts, a gazebo and huts, two flagpoles and a lake. The camp was pretty and smelled good, like fresh air after a storm, even though there was no storm—the sun was blazing, and it was hot.

When he'd gotten off the bus, grabbing his stuff and making a run for it had seemed like the best thing to do. Listening to counselors shouting names of hills and cabins he'd never heard of had made him feel out of place, and he thought it would be nice to hold on to his baseball mitt, if not his dignity. But, of course, Bobby hadn't found the mitt—his mom had buried it somewhere at the bottom of his duffel—and here he was, wandering around alone, following weathered, unreadable signs for Boys' Side.

He reached into the front pocket of his hoodie and brought a folded note to his nose. It smelled familiar, like his mom's perfume. As the fragrance loitered in his nostrils, he wished he was home, watching TV on the couch. Bobby breathed out of his nose, blowing the misleading sense of comfort from his body, along with a little snot. Misleading, because he knew it was light-years away from the anger he'd felt toward his mom this morning when she'd given him the boot.

Robert,
    Just a reminder—the name of your cabin is San Juan Hill. The camp directors told me you're going to really like the boys in your age group. Have a fun bus ride! And don't forget to write.
    xo,
    Mom

Bobby crumpled up the note, shoved it back into his pocket, and kept moving. When he was three-quarters up the biggest of the four big hills (he now knew where the name "Rolling Hills" came from), he heard voices over a loudspeaker. The sound echoed from behind him and above him and below him.

Grown-up Guy: Good morning, Camp Rolling Hills! Can I get a *Rrrroooollling* Hills? Welcome, or welcome back— whichever it is, you're welcome! We're pumped like limitless ketchup that you are here with us *ahora*. This is going to be an *amaaaa*—
Woman: TJ! You're gonna break the mic . . .
Same Guy = TJ: —*zing* summer!
Woman: So much to do—no time to waste!

TJ: So find your counselors, and make haste!

Woman: Dinner's at six today—

TJ [*butchering an Italian accent*]: A'spaghetti and a'meat-balls.

Woman: I'd have abs of steel if they weren't so irresistibly delicious.

TJ: Oh, Captain, you do have abs of—

The loudspeaker went off with a sharp squeal of feedback. Bobby took it that TJ and the Captain ran the camp. That, or they were staff who'd hijacked the loudspeaker system. It really could be either.

Bobby spotted a cabin up ahead with SAN JUAN HILL etched into a piece of driftwood nailed above the door. He was glad he'd arrived, even though he was nervous to meet his cabinmates and totally confused by the name of the cabin. He knew San Juan was in Puerto Rico, but they weren't in Puerto Rico. They were in upstate New York. The "Hill" part, he got.

He wiped the sweat from his forehead and ran his fingers through his hair. The Surf Hair he'd applied that morning made his hair look like he'd just gotten out of the ocean, and it smelled like the piña coladas his mom would drink when family vacations had still been a thing. Bobby might've felt lousy about being here, but he didn't want to look it.

He lugged his duffel up the four . . . five . . . six porch steps to where five more duffels were piled beside the door. *How'd they get here so fast?* he wondered. The other campers must've used a shortcut.

A small kid, even smaller than Bobby, stuck his head—well, really, his entire torso—out the cabin window. "We've got a new kid!" he cried. The window suddenly slammed shut on him, and he laugh-cried in pain, wriggling back inside.

Bobby hurried to help him, but four boys and a teenager with a STAFF shirt rushed out of the cabin, blocking his way. And . . . they were *chanting*.

"We welcome you to Rolling Hills.
We roll, you roll with us.
If loyal to your cabinmates,
We're glad to add a plus!"

One kid with a curly 'fro was lounging on Bobby's duffel like it was a reclining beach chair. Bobby itched to say, *Get up! You're crushing my stuff!* But he didn't want to make the kid feel bad. Bobby's gaze darted from one guy to the next. It was all the same: relentless enthusiasm, all focused on him. He'd never had to avoid so much eye contact in his life.

At last there was silence. He felt relief course through his body. The chant was finally—

"Camp Rolling Hills
Our home for e'er, you'll be . . ."

False alarm. Bobby bit his lip to distract himself from the pressing panic in his chest as he observed Act Two: a song. In harmony. The boys' hands were over their hearts.

The anxiety rolling in his stomach made him think back to that morning, when his mom had ambushed him with one of his pills over breakfast. "Mine is mellow yellow, yours is baby-boy blue," she'd said, placing their medications side by side like they were friends.

"But Dad said I don't have to take them over the summer," he'd argued at the time. Neither Bobby nor his dad wanted him to be pinpointed as the pill-popping newbie with diagnosed freak-out issues.

"Look, honey, I don't know what sets you off, and that makes me very nervous. You of all people should understand the power of nerves."

Now Bobby glanced up at the singing guys and felt his left eye twitch. His mom was right. He did understand the power of nerves. And he wished more than anything that he didn't—that he could be normal, like his dad. Not victim to Bizarro Bobby (the name he'd given to his anxiety, after Superman's Bizarro, an evil doppelgänger from another dimension trying to take him down). He hated how he had to fight heart palpitations that made him feel like he was about to die.

Meanwhile, the guys were still singing.

"In the bosom of the valley
Sun shines over thee."

Each of the guys pounded his heart with his right hand, turned his fist into a peace sign, and then moved the peace sign over his head like a rainbow.

Bobby gripped the short hair on the back of his head to steady himself but tried to make it look like he was giving it a *No big deal* scratch. Somehow, stupidly, he'd convinced his mom he didn't need the pills at camp. That he would be totally fine, and she could always send them up. But that was before he was about to freak in front of a bunch of guys he was stuck with for seven weeks plus three and a half days, and all before they even knew his name. He should've downed the tablet with his Eggos and pocketed the rest.

"Camp Rolling Hills,
Firm our loyalty . . ."

Bobby had hoped to slip under the radar here or, at best, to blend in. Not sung at with the merciless pep of a choir straight out of *Glee*. He took three deep breaths in an attempt to resist Bizarro. Thankfully, Bizarro Bobby seemed to be staying put for now, sort of the way his pup, Clark Kent, did when he hunted squirrels. He didn't go away, he just waited patiently for the right time to pounce.

"May our hearts be filled forever
With thy memories."

The guys were just standing there now, and Bobby almost clapped, having no idea what the protocol was for whatever had just happened. But before he could do anything, they all charged at him, lifted him up over their heads, and carried him inside.

Bobby felt the color in his face drain to a ghostly gray. His parents must have accidentally signed him up for a cult. He should call them to let them know, but, oh yeah, he remembered: no cell phones allowed. In a final blow, his mom had snatched his only connection to the outside world on the way out of the house.

"Hey, hey, let the kid down easy," said the guy in the STAFF shirt. Bobby was grateful that someone had his back. He'd been emotionally preparing himself for broken bones—already picturing the white casts, doodle- and signature-free. Physical reminders of his broken life and friendless summer.

His feet crashed to the floor first, and he found himself standing dizzily, trying not to wobble. A big kid was next to him, and, without asking permission, Bobby held his shoulder for support until he was sure he wouldn't fall over.

"What's your name, buddy?" the counselor asked as the other boys went to the porch to collect their bags.

"Robert," he answered. His friends called him Bobby, but he was sure these guys were nothing like them. Keith and Jake didn't sing. And they certainly didn't sing *at* him. Unless it was his birthday, and even then Bobby made sure the Happy Birthday song was sung on the DL.

As the five other campers dragged their duffels into the cabin, Bobby slowly regained his composure and took a look around. Three unmade wooden bunk-beds were pushed against the walls with empty cubbies, shelves, and plastic dressers in between. In the far left corner was an open curtain, replacing what could've been a door. He moved forward to get a better view of what was inside.

"Yup, that's Rick's nook. I'm Rick. It's my nook," said the counselor.

Inside was a hammock with pillows. Jeans and T-shirts were strewn on the floor, and a dark red tapestry of an elephant was nailed to the wall. Right outside the nook was a guitar, propped against the foot of a bunk-bed. Bobby's mind drifted to his dad and the story about how he'd taught himself to play guitar in college so he could win over the girl who later became Bobby's mom. *That worked out well in the end*, Bobby thought sarcastically.

"You play?" Rick asked, watching Bobby scope out his stuff.

"Oh. No."

"Well, listen, welcome to Camp Rolling Hills."

As if I didn't get a chant and a song already.

"And I know it's your first day, but just so you know for the future, you've gotta stay with the group. What we do, you do." Rick was feeding Bobby's cult suspicions.

"Sorry. I had to get my bag, and then I got lost . . ."

"You didn't know they bring the bags for you?" Big Kid blurted out, his mouth full of sandwich. He rolled his duffel in front of him, crashing whatever was inside with every push.

"Nah, didn't know." *If I did, I wouldn't have dragged my duffel up four enormous hills*, Bobby thought but didn't dare say.

"No prob," Rick assured him, pulling Bobby's duffel inside and using his right Birkenstock to keep the door from slamming shut. "Guys, help the newbie with his stuff. Show him how neatly you all unpack."

"I color-coordinate my shirts on occasion," bragged the small kid who'd nearly been hacked in two by the window, "just so I really know what my options are when I get dressed in the morning." Big Kid dumped Small Kid's clothes on the floor. "Come on!" Small Kid whined.

Bobby looked to Rick, expecting him to make Big Kid drop and give him twenty, like at baseball camp.

Instead, Rick clapped his hands together. "All right. Cubby your folded clothes."

Do what *to your folded clothes?*

"Start strong, boys. I'll be out on the porch if anyone needs me."

Rick slipped outside, and Big Kid nodded in sync with the sound of the door slamming shut. "Shot top bunk!" he hollered, climbing to the top of the bunk-bed closest to the window.

"No way, Play Dough! You can't have top bunk—you'll crush me," whined Small Kid, groping Big Kid's ankles.

Bobby took note: Big Kid's name was Play Dough. At least, that was his cult name.

"No, I won't."

"Deriving a conclusion based on simple physics, you will," replied an Asian kid with lab goggles around his neck.

"Fine," Big Kid/Play Dough said. "Then, Wiener"—he indicated the Small Kid—"as the baby of the cabin, you can bunk with New Kid." Bobby couldn't tell if they were punishing *him* for being new or Wiener for being young, or both.

"I'll be twelve soon," Wiener protested.

"Yeah, like, next year. Steinberg will sleep below me," said Play Dough, looking at Asian Kid.

"Can't. Asthma. The dust."

Wiener swaggered toward Bobby, pushing out his inverted chest. "Hey, New Kid! I gotta be on bottom for easy access. So, climb on top like a cop."

Before Bobby gave up the bottom bunk to this little guy, the butt of the cabin's jokes, he wanted to make sure he wasn't getting the raw end of the deal. "Easy access to what?"

"To the bathroom. He's a bed wetter," joked Play Dough.

He'd better be joking, thought Bobby. *It would stink, like, actually stink, to sleep above a bed wetter.*

"No!" Wiener objected. "It's 'cause I gotta have easy access to the back door, so I can sneak out to visit my girlfriend."

"Dude-a-cris, you don't have a girlfriend," Play Dough said.

Asian Kid/Steinberg nodded like he dug it. "'Dude-a-cris'? Cool."

"Well, maybe this summer I will," Wiener said, exhaling into his palm and smelling his breath.

"We've watched you try with almost every girl our age," Play Dough continued. "Not gonna happen."

"Uh, my voice is deeper now. And at least I try, instead of pining and whining and doing nothing about it like you."

"I don't whine," Play Dough whined.

"All I'm saying is, this summer we're supposed to go for girls. That's what you do in Upper Camp, right?" Wiener cocked his chin at Bobby.

Bobby looked over his shoulder, sure that Wiener must be asking someone who actually knew what he was talking about.

"Plus, did you see Melman? Holy turds, she got hot."

"'Holy turds'?" Steinberg asked.

"Yeah, I'm trying it."

"Don't," said Play Dough.

"Which one is Melman?" Bobby asked. He wondered if she was the pretty girl from the bus who'd lost her pencils.

"Baseball hat, cargo shorts," said Play Dough.

Negative, Bobby decided. The girl from the bus had been wearing jean shorts. And if she'd been sporting a baseball cap, Bobby definitely would've noticed.

"Melman has the most penetrating eyes." Wiener sighed dreamily, picking up a stack of his T-shirts from the floor.

Bobby couldn't believe how weird these guys talked.

"'Penetrating,' how?" asked a kid wearing a Nike sweatband. He brushed past with a hockey stick, a lacrosse stick, and a baseball bat tucked under his arm.

"They were shooting Wiener warning glances to stay back at least a hundred feet," Play Dough joked.

Wiener seemed to enjoy the attention, but Bobby would hate to be shot down every time he said something, even if it was by his friends and even if most of what he was saying was really annoying.

"No, they were inviting me in—I could tell."

"You're gonna go inside her eye? That's impossible," said Nike Sweatband.

Curly 'Fro—the kid who'd lounged on Bobby's duffel—

jumped down from his top bunk. A compass and a stick of natural deodorant came down with him. "Totle's got a point. I think she wears contacts," he said.

Bobby took note: Big Kid was Play Dough. Small Kid was Wiener. Asian Kid was, improbably, Steinberg. Nike Sweatband was Totle. Curly 'Fro was the only one left.

With the whole penetrating-eyes argument cleared up, the guys went back to their unpacking. Wiener picked up more piles of clothes from the floor. Steinberg shook his inhaler. Bobby unzipped his duffel. He hoped Curly 'Fro hadn't actually crushed anything important when he'd lounged on top of it. He was lean but muscle-y.

Play Dough strolled over to Bobby. "You see what I have to deal with here, New Kid? It's our fourth year, and it's the same thing every summer."

"It's Robert," Bobby reminded Play Dough.

For some reason, Wiener got really excited at that. So excited, he accidentally elbowed his cologne off a plastic dresser. "Yo, Play Dough! Did you hear this kid's name?"

"Yeah, Robert. We all heard it, brain-clog."

"But . . . I'm Robert at home," Steinberg objected, unloading batteries from his JanSport backpack.

"Well, what's your last name?" Totle asked Bobby.

"Benjamin."

"But my first name is Benjamin!" Curly 'Fro exclaimed.

"Yeah, we can't have that. You're gonna need a nickname." Play Dough sat Bobby down on a thin, plastic mattress, his chunky arm around Bobby's shoulders. He seemed serious about it, which made Bobby a little nervous. But it was OK, he told himself. He'd had nicknames before: Rob, Robbie, Bob, Bobby (his first choice), and Bobert (his last choice). *Please, no one call me Bobert*, he prayed.

"Steinberg, why don't you start it off?" Play Dough said.

"Sure thing." Steinberg took the lead like he'd done this before, like it was just another cult ritual everyone was in on. "OK, New Kid, I understand your name is Robert, and it's . . . interesting that my name is Robert, too, but because we're both Robert . . ."

"I need a nickname—got it, yeah."

"Plus, Robert's the type of name that stunts your potential."

Stunts my potential for what? Bobby wondered.

"It doesn't get you far," Play Dough explained.

He wanted to fight back, defend the Robert inside him, but Play Dough was right. *Robert* hadn't gotten him anywhere. It was the name his mom called him when they were running late for therapy, and the name his dad called him when he wanted to have a man-to-man talk about how he and Bobby's mom were "taking a break." Bobby's stomach started to knot.

"But *Steinberg* isn't a nickname," Curly 'Fro said. "It's just your last name."

"Dude, *Dover* is your nickname and your last name," Play Dough pointed out.

"Touché."

"Your name is Ben Dover?" Bobby asked.

"Yup."

"No way," Bobby said with a touch of sympathy. *Ben Dover*

was the alias he'd used for prank calls with Keith and Jake back in fifth grade, when they'd dial random numbers and try to sell people their used underwear.

"You'll never guess where mine comes from," Play Dough said. He left zero time for Bobby to guess. "You see, at school people call me Fat Brian Garfink."

Is he waiting for me to tell him he's not fat? Bobby wondered. "You're not—"

"It's cool. I get paid to run on treadmills."

"Who pays you, your mom?" Wiener cracked.

"Uh, yeah." Play Dough turned back to Bobby. "I like to eat. A lot."

"You should see him go," added Steinberg. "He'll eat anything. Last Visiting Day, he ate an entire cookie cake. He's also eaten a five-day-old egg-salad sandwich."

"Ewwww . . ." Bobby didn't get grossed out easily, but the thought of hot, rotten, old egg salad was too much.

"I found it under my mattress," Play Dough added proudly. "So, one day we went hiking, and I got lost, 'cause I was looking at a rock—"

"Why were you looking—"

"ADHD," inserted Steinberg.

Ah, thought Bobby.

"I wandered around alone for, like, five hours, *so* hungry. I finally found my way back, but by then I had missed Dinner and Snack and had eaten all my stashed Gushers and Kudos the week before, so I had nothing."

"Then he threatened to eat me!" Wiener screeched, now accidentally knocking his pyramid of hair gel containers to the floor.

"Don't exaggerate."

"You bit my arm!"

"It had sweat on it. Sweat is salt, right, Steinberg?" "Sweat is urine that comes out of your pores," Steinberg said.

Ew, gross. As the conversation got weirder and weirder, Bobby could feel his stomach knotting further—twisting and turning. He sweat a lot, especially in the summer, and double-especially in new environments. He prayed these guys wouldn't start cracking jokes about how he was soaked in pee.

"Exactly," said Play Dough. "Why drink Wiener's pee, when I had just received a care package?" He faced Bobby. "It was right there on my bed. From my Aunt Hessie, who thinks I'm five and who makes clay kittens in her basement."

"But it wasn't food," Steinberg explained.

"She'd sent me Play-Doh."

"You . . . ate the Play-Doh?" Bobby guessed.

"Yup."

"They say it's nontoxic"—Steinberg smirked—"but the label's a lie."

"I sprinted for the can and—"

"Pooped out a rainbow!" the bunk exclaimed in unison, all laughing maniacally.

Bobby wanted to cringe. Not because it was gross, but because they were laughing so loud, so close, it hurt his ears. Play Dough had eaten Play-Doh. That was all they'd needed to say. What was the matter with these guys?

Bobby focused on Totle, who was taping up a New York Jets poster by his bed. He seemed to be the normalest of the bunch and could be a potential ally. Maybe his name came from something less weird than eating rainbow-colored clay. "OK, so what about you?" Bobby asked. "Totle's your name or your nickname?"

"All men by nature desire to know," Totle responded, stroking an invisible beard.

Never mind. Bobby's heart sank.

"My name's Justin. I was named for my great-uncle, also named Justin. But Justin is a boring name, and I'm kind of philosophic."

"Philosophical," Steinberg corrected.

"Whatever." Totle took a deep breath through his nose. It whistled. "So, at first we tried out Plato."

"But that was way too confusing," said Play Dough. "Pla*to*, Play *Dough*."

"We considered Socrates, but Justin's more Aristotelian," Steinberg explained, his lab goggles now tightly fastened to his face. "But *Aristotle* is mad hard to say, you know? Try saying it seven times."

Bobby nodded in agreement, but then he noticed they were all looking at him, actually waiting for him to say it. "Uh, Aristotle, Aristotle, Aristotle, Aristotle, Ar-stotle, Ar-stot-le, Ari—"

"Exactly," Steinberg cut in, gesturing to Totle.

"So we shortened it to Totle!"

"Steinberg, do me!" Wiener said excitedly, leaping from his bed and bringing his entire plastic dresser down with him. "Best for last."

Steinberg cocked his head in disagreement. "His name is Ernest Meyer."

Totle chuckled with a bit of a snort. "Yeah, his name is really *Ernest!*"

"So . . . ?" Wiener said.

Bobby was with him on this one. Since when was Ernest a funny name?

"Anyway, he begged us to call him Ernie, so how could we not call him Bert?" said Steinberg.

"But Bert was acting all grouchy, so we switched his name to Oscar," Play Dough added, looking at Bobby to see if he was following. He was.

"That made him Oscar Mayer," Steinberg continued. "You know, the *hot dog* guy . . . ?"

"Yeah."

"That's how I'm Wiener!"

He seemed thrilled with a nickname that would make any other kid sink with humiliation. *Maybe brainwashing is part of the cult*, Bobby thought. He wanted no part of it.

"All right, New Robert, what's your middle name?" Play Dough asked, getting down to business.

"Ernest."

"Ernest! No way!" Wiener raised his hand for a high five.

Play Dough slapped Wiener's hand down before Bobby could high-five him back.

"OK, people"—Steinberg clapped—"we need some plan-B inspiration."

That was all he needed to say before the questions flooded

in faster than Bobby could answer. Faster than he could think.

"Do you have any mad skills?"

"Quirky hobbies?"

"Go-to movie quotes?"

"Go-to normal quotes that, like, people say?"

"What's your favorite tool in the toolbox?"

"Do you have a spirit animal?"

"Where are you from?"

Finally, a pause. Bobby didn't know what "mad skills" meant, he didn't have any quirky hobbies, and he couldn't think of movie quotes on the spot or any quotes, for that matter. He guessed he liked hammers, but that was boring, and he had his cockapoo, Clark Kent, but Clark wasn't a spirit animal—whatever that was—he was real, so Bobby wasn't sure that counted.

Then again, Bobby didn't want to answer these questions, anyway. They were personal and no one's business, and if he did say "hammer" or "cockapoo," would his nickname be "Hammer" or "Cockapoo" all summer? Plus, he didn't understand why he couldn't claim any of the obvious nicknames for Robert. This all seemed like a lot of work for no reason.

Eventually he settled on an answer. "Well . . . I'm from New Jersey."

"New Jersey? I've been there. It smells funny," declared Dover, like he was the first person to notice.

"Do you smell funny?" asked Play Dough, giving Bobby a sniff.

Bobby held his breath, trying not to release any more stink.

He'd already sweat (not peed) through his blue T-shirt. It was navy now.

"Hey! That's it! Smelly!" Steinberg yelped, without giving Play Dough a chance to confirm that Bobby didn't smell, even though he probably did. They all did, it was really hot.

"'Smelly'?" Wiener mulled that over.

Bobby thought about how, if he were Wiener, he'd be relieved the new kid was about to get stuck with a nickname that, by comparison, made his nickname the coolest name ever. But then again, Bobby wasn't brainwashed. Everyone looked to Play Dough.

"Smelly!" he pronounced.

"Smelly!!!" the guys cheered.

Bobby threw up a little in his mouth and forced it back down. He couldn't believe he was really going to have to go by "Smelly" all summer at this stupid, weird camp with these stupid, weird people all because his mom's stupid weirdness was pushing his dad away. He just wanted to be called Bobby by his real friends, Keith and Jake, who went by their real names, Keith and Jake, like normal people.

Play Dough picked up a broom. "Kneel, Robert of Jersey . . ." He pushed Bobby down by his head. He tapped him on his right shoulder, then swept the broom over his head to the left one.

Steinberg whispered, in gibberish, some sort of strange blessing. *"Kvetch, tuches, goyish, oy vey, mazel tov!"*

Play Dough nodded to him and continued. "Arise, Sir Smelly!"

"Guys, I really don't—"

"Smelly!!!" they cheered over him.

"Does it have to be Smelly?" Bobby's anxiety bubbled in his stomach, and his face burned. "Let's talk about this. We can come up with something better, can't we?" He hid his trembling hands. He could feel the onset of panic in his chest. "How about 'Jersey'?"

The guys marched around the cabin, climbing bunk-beds, jumping off bunk-beds, army-crawling on the floor, chanting wildly, "Sme-lly! Sme-lly! Sme-lly!"

Bobby had doubted they could get any more enthusiastic than when they'd sung their welcome song, but that was just the warm-up. His head felt cloudy and dizzy, and he was losing himself to Bizarro Bobby by the second.

"Sme-lly! Sme-lly! Sme-lly!"

Bobby didn't care how much they loved nicknames in their freaky cult, he just wished they'd leave him out of it. Or at least not parade around the room like psychos, mocking him, singling him out, and stripping him of what little dignity he had left. "I'm totally cool with the limitations of Robert!" he yelled out in one last attempt.

It didn't stop. Bizarro reveled in his vicious attack as the boys cheered louder and louder.

There was no janitor's closet in sight, like at school, and Bobby needed to be alone. Away from the taunting "Sme-lly!" chant, away from these weirdos, away from all of it. *I need to escape, to hide, to be anywhere but here. Just away. Far, far away,* he repeated in his head. Bobby found himself dumping everything from his oversize duffel onto the floor, laying the bag out on a bottom bunk, climbing inside, and zipping himself in as best he could.

He closed his eyes, trying to think about good stuff, like Keith and Jake and his other friends who called him Bobby, and Clark Kent's bark, which scared the squirrels, and Keith's Purim carnival, where he'd won Goldie the Goldfish, and the game he'd played with All-Star Louis Fenderson at baseball camp. Bobby wished he could go back in time to when his dad had changed his life by introducing him to the Beatles on his iPod. It all seemed so far away.

Suddenly, the sound of unzippering broke through his swirling thoughts.

"Hey, buddy, you got yourself stuck in there?"

Bobby opened his eyes, and there stood Rick, his shaggy hair falling to the sides of his face. Bobby had no idea how long he'd been daydreaming. Thirty seconds? Ten minutes? He was so humiliated, he could die.

"Nah, just chilling," Bobby said casually, as if it were totally normal for him to be stuffed inside a duffel bag at his own doing.

"All right. Well, I'm gonna get started refolding your clothes. Wanna give me a hand?"

Bobby nodded, and as Rick pulled him out of the duffel, he tried to prepare himself for the judge-y stares and the *You have a nice nap in your suitcase?* jokes the guys were surely cracking.

But to his surprise, they didn't even seem to notice. Totle was busy tossing his clothes into his cubby like it was a basketball hoop, Steinberg cleaned his lab goggles with toilet paper,

Dover draped a Boy Scout sash filled with merit badges over the foot of his top bunk, Wiener color-coordinated his clothes, and Play Dough ate a Slim Jim from a stash hidden in his sock. No more chanting. No more singing. No more unwanted attention.

In fact, no one seemed fazed by Bobby's freak-out at all. He couldn't tell if he was more relieved or weirded out.

"You want these T-shirts here?" Rick asked, pointing to an empty cubby against the wall.

Since he couldn't go home and he couldn't hide, he might as well unpack. "Yeah," he said. Bobby was sure the worst summer of his life had officially begun.

Icebreakers

"Would you like some sugar in your tea?" Melman asked Slimey in her supposedly British accent.

Slimey fell into a giggling fit atop Harold Hill, tugging at the grass to steady herself. Melman had been speaking in that accent since the glorious reunion of the "fraternal twins" two hours ago, but she came off sounding more like a sophisticated pirate.

Slimey took a deep breath and watched the sun turn the sky a cotton-candy pink. It was so good to be back, waiting for their first Evening Activity. "Hate to break it to you, but that is so *not* how British people talk. Haven't you seen *Harry Potter?*"

"*Harry Potter* isn't real life. I'm real life!!!" Melman shouted in her "British" accent again, this time sounding like a drowning wizard with two broken hearing aids. Her hands flailed in the golden sky as she danced circles around Slimey, the two of them drawing *What the what?* glances from their cabinmates scattered around the hill. Melman was being her normal, insane self.

"I've missed your weirdness!"

"You should have visited me after school," she joked, plopping down on the grass beside Slimey. "London's, like, only five minutes from Teaneck, New Jersey."

Slimey wished that were true. She wished Melman's dad hadn't gotten transferred overseas in September, taking her best friend in the whole world with him. "Nah, Skyping was way more fun."

"You're right. We should just Skype at camp—walk around with laptops. We'd never have to real-life see each other again!" Melman scooted closer and threw her arms around Slimey's neck. "Oh, Slimes, I'm really glad you came back. I don't think I could handle the J-squad without you."

Slimey looked over her shoulder at Jenny braiding Jamie's hair on the other side of the hill. Missi was there, too, and Slimey watched her creep her fingers through Jenny's hair, only to be shot down by the J-squad's unified stare-glare. Sophie was in the middle of the hill, throwing grass at the sky and whispering in Latin or Chinese or something. Sara hadn't let her bring a book along, even though she could've read a whole chapter at this point—the boys were super-late.

"Earth to Slimey," Melman said.

Slimey turned back to face her. "Of course I came back to camp. Why wouldn't I?"

"I don't know. Bad memories?"

A lump formed in Slimey's throat. She reached around her neck for her silver locket, really needing to open and close it at this very moment, but it wasn't there. She knew no one was allowed to wear jewelry during Activity Periods, but taking it off for the first time in ten months was like separating from

Teddy the teddy bear when she was two, except much worse. She hoped it was safe where she'd left it—on the underside of Melman's top bunk, dangling above her Mooshi pillow. She felt naked without it on and didn't know what to do with her hands. She dug her fingernails into her stomach.

"The bad memories are at home, too."

"I know, but, like, you found out right in the—"

"I know where I found out, Melman," Slimey cut in. "Being at home is worse. There're pictures of him, and all his clothes are still in the closet, and my mom, you know, is . . ." Her voice cracked, and she couldn't say another word without tearing up, and she didn't want to tear up, not now, so she stopped.

"Yeah," Melman whispered gently, taking Slimey's hand from her stomach and giving it a tight squeeze.

"Here, at least, I have the locket he gave me, and I have you. I'll be fine," Slimey assured her, squeezing her hand back. The lump in her throat was still there, but it wasn't choking her anymore. It was just a little stuck.

"Together we'll make it the best summer ever—you'll see," Melman said, bringing back the British accent, pulling Slimey up and twirling her around.

Slimey let Melman twirl her over and over again. It made her laugh, which freed up the lump, even if it didn't come close to filling the hole in her heart.

Slimey was dizzy in a good way when she heard Sara un-enthusiastically delivering instructions. "Line up, ladies, all in one place." Melman and Slimey wobbled over to where Sara and Sophie were waiting. "The San Juan boys have finally decided to grace us with their presence, and we might as well look ready," she droned.

"Why?" asked Jamie, shuffling her feet lazily.

"To make them feel bad for being late."

"Missi, come stand between us," Jenny purred sweetly, even though it was obvious she was manipulating the order (and Missi's feelings) so that if they counted off every other girl to make teams, she and Jamie would be together.

The boys charged up Harold Hill like a mischievous troop of monkeys: jumping, pushing one another, and laughing. Slimey was pretty sure Play Dough was eating a banana. But . . . now that he was getting closer, she could see it was a slice of lemon cake. Steinberg sprinted past him but didn't get too far before he had to stop and puff his inhaler. Totle reached the girls first, pulling his T-shirt over his head and hopping from foot to foot, his signature victory dance. Dover arrived next and jogged straight past their line, his palm up for high fives. The girls all gave him one, except for Jamie and Jenny, who just looked at him skeptically, and Sophie, who stabbed her pointer finger into his hand instead. Somehow, Wiener had snuck in front of Melman and Slimey. He performed a set of push-ups, starting his count at one hundred and only making it to a hundred and three before he collapsed onto the grass.

Rick, pulling up the rear, greeted the two cabin groups with his typical intense enthusiasm. "All right, Anita Hill ladies and San Juan gents, find yourselves a partner of the opposite sex!"

No one moved. It wasn't that they didn't want to be paired up, but what Rick didn't understand was that they weren't ten anymore. Whoever you chose meant A LOT at this age. If a girl approached a guy to be her partner, she might as well be asking him to the Midsummer Dance.

"Come on, guys . . . ," Rick said, his pressing stare hopping from camper to camper.

Slimey looked at the boys spread around the hill, heads down and kicking dirt—all the hyperness knocked right out of them. She thought about walking over to Dover, since he was passionate about random activities and only three paces away, but since she didn't want to make any misleading statements the first night of camp, she took Melman's hand instead.

"Really? OK, then, I guess Sara and I will match you up ourselves." Rick looked to his co-counselor for support. "Sara?"

"Rick?" she shot back icily, making no move to help.

Slimey didn't know why Sara was acting so cold. As far as she knew, nothing had happened in the last half a day to make Sara upset. Plus, Rick was Sara's boyfriend's best friend, and they had all grown up together at camp.

"All right, then, here we go." Rick rubbed his hands together as the campers stood frozen with anticipation.

Slimey was still standing beside Melman, and if she couldn't be paired off with her, then she guessed any boy would be fine. She knew Melman didn't care who she was with, either, as long as it wasn't Wiener.

"Wiener with Melman," Rick announced.

"Score!" shouted Wiener, throwing a celebratory fist into the air. Melman shook her head at him. Undiscouraged, he yawned and stretched his arm so that it hovered above her shoulders.

Dumbest. Move. Ever. Luckily, Melman was a pro and smoothly ducked out of the way before any physical contact could be made.

"Play Dough and Jamie," Rick announced, looking at Jenny.

"I'm Jenny. She's Jamie."

"Are you sure?"

"What? Yes! I'm Jenny—"

"*She's* Jenny," Rick confirmed, looking at Jamie.

"No!" Jenny cried out.

Of course Rick knows who we are, Slimey thought with a smile. Rick had known them all since they were One Tree Hillers and he was a Counselor-in-Training. He used to let them take turns riding on his shoulders while he ran as fast as he could.

"They're basically the same person," Sophie explained, not picking up on the fact that Rick was kidding, "except Jenny tells Jamie what to do, and she does it, and Jamie asks Jenny what to do, and she tells her."

"It was a joke, Sophie! We three may be besties, but that doesn't mean he can't tell us apart," Missi chimed in, throwing her wiry arms over the J-squad's shoulders. It was painful to watch her relentless third-wheeling.

Rick rattled off the rest of the pairs. "Totle and Jenny, Steinberg and Sophie, Dover and Missi, Smelly and Slimey."

Smelly? Slimey wondered. *Who's Rick calling Smelly? And why am I—*

That's when she saw him, stepping out from behind Play Dough. In a blue T-shirt, red shorts, and a gray hoodie—same outfit from the bus. He was shorter than she thought he'd be but just as cute, with tousled brown hair and those same warm brown eyes. He looked up, and Slimey waved. *Don't talk too much, Slimey*, she reminded herself. *Just act normal.* She knew she should just act like he was Play Dough or Steinberg or Dover, even. Guys she'd only seen as friends. She didn't want to ruin it the way she'd ruined her chances at school with Peter by talking too much about Ron Weasley.

He half smiled as they walked toward each other. "So you're . . . ?"

"Slimey, yeah."

"Cool. Nice to—"

"You're from New Jersey!" she exclaimed. *Take it down a notch, Slimey.*

"Oh. Yeah . . ."

"I recognize you from the Paramus bus."

"Oh!" he said, relieved. "Right! I picked up your—"

"I didn't stalk you or anything."

"No, I didn't think that."

"OK, good."

"We're both from New Jersey—cool. Where, um . . . where in—"

"OK, San Juan-*itas*," Rick interrupted, "time for the first game of the night. Before we get started, I want you to turn to your partner and tell each other one random thing about yourself. On your mark, get set—"

"Do I have to stay with Totle?" Jenny whined.

"Yes," Sara answered.

"No," Rick overlapped.

The counselors exchanged a look. Slimey kind of agreed with Sara. If she were Totle, she wouldn't want to be rejected, even if it meant getting a nicer partner. Jenny and Jamie switched guys anyway, and since Totle didn't seem to care, and Play Dough seemed happier paired with Jenny, Slimey turned back to Boy from the Bus. She wished she'd spent the last minute thinking about what to say instead of worrying about the boys. Now she was bound to go off on a nervous tangent. "So, random fact. Do you wanna go first?"

"Sure. Is Slimey a nickname?" he asked.

Good. Now I have something to talk about! she thought, relieved. "Well, yeah, that's what everyone calls me."

"Oh. I bet you can get them to call you something else, like, uh, Cool . . . Cat, since you're not slimy."

"Thanks." She giggled. "But I actually like Slimey. I wish I was called it at school instead of Stephanie Gregson, 'cause there's, like, three Stephanies in my grade." *Does he think I'm cool? Or just as cool as a cat?* She thought cats were cool, but not as cool as cockatiels.

"Where did it come from?"

"Oh, so when I was eight, I was a little dyslexic, but not really, and my grandparents used to call me 'Smiley' in their letters. So when I wrote back, I signed off 'Love, Slimey' instead of 'Smiley,' and it was funny, and it stuck."

"Cool."

He thinks I'm cool! she cheered herself on. "So, what's your real name, Smelly?"

"Yeah, I was hoping you missed that when Rick was pairing us off. It's Robert. The guys are calling me Smelly—but I don't smell, I swear—so they should really just call me Bobby."

"OK, Bobby." Slimey took a sneaky whiff, and he was right—he didn't smell bad at all. In fact, he smelled like piña coladas.

Rick clapped to get their attention. "All right, now that you've learned some random info, let's move on to a Camp Rolling Hills favorite. Each pair is going to get one of these marshmallows on a licorice string."

"Sweet-sauce!" Play Dough exclaimed.

"Do *not* eat the marshmallow."

"Sour-sauce!"

"Each partner is going to take an end of the string and put it in their mouth. When I say go, you start eating. Whoever gets to the marshmallow first wins!"

Bobby looked confused. Slimey figured he'd never played this game before, and she was suddenly jittery-excited to show him how it was done.

Rick waited a split second, and then: "On your mark, get set, go!"

Slimey went at it, chewing the licorice as fast as she could. She looked at Bobby's face getting closer and closer to hers, and then she looked up at his hair to avoid eye contact. She noticed he was doing the same. Her lips closed around the marshmallow. "Yes, I win!" Slimey took the marshmallow out of her mouth, sucking her saliva off it. "Want a bite?"

Bobby crossed his arms. "Uh, it was already in your mouth."

"It's camp. We share everything."

"That's . . . weird."

No, it's not, Slimey thought. *It's not like I have the stomach flu.* A little hurt, she put the marshmallow back in her mouth and chewed. It didn't taste so good anymore. It would be a million times better if it were roasted. She bet he'd share it with her then.

"Sorry. I didn't mean it like that," he said, uncrossing his arms. "I guess I just have a lot to get used to."

His apology gave the marshmallow some of its flavor back. "Well, how do you like camp so far?"

"It's . . . fine."

Fine? No one describes camp as fine. Amazing, incredible, life-changing, *maybe. But never* fine.

"The first time I came here," she offered, "it took me a couple of days to realize how much I loved it, but once you do, you love it forever. You'll see."

"That would be cool, to love camp. For this summer, at least. Next summer, my parents told me I could go back to baseball camp and play All-Stars."

But everyone comes back to camp. No matter what, she thought. "Cool . . . ," she said instead.

"Yeah, I didn't want to come here, but my parents are . . . not getting along, and they wanted the summer to sort stuff out. Baseball camp's only three weeks."

Slimey could feel her heart tighten in her chest. She got it now. Bobby hadn't come here because he'd begged his mom to let him, the way she had. He was forced away because stuff at home was bad. That explained his rudeness. "Oh. I'm sorry. About your parents, I mean."

"Yeah, well . . ."

"I know this isn't baseball camp, but when things are tough at home, isn't it nice to just be away?"

Bobby smiled and shook his head.

She wasn't sure if he was disagreeing or agreeing. She hoped he agreed.

"I was thinking the same thing."

He agrees!

"I miss home a little, but I don't know how much more of it I could've handled."

"Yeah, that makes sense." Slimey loved spending time with her mom, but sometimes it was hard to cheer her up when she wished she could crumble in her mom's arms instead of her mom crumbling in hers. "Anyway, camp is weird. It might take a couple of days to like it, or sometimes it hits you when you're home at the end of the summer, and you're, like, 'Wow, that was amazing. I'm reverse homesick—I'm camp-sick.' And then you can't stop thinking about it and feeling this very real feeling, you know?"

Bobby nodded. His eyes had a little bit of caramel in them, she noticed.

"I'm not saying it's definitely gonna be like that for you, but maybe you'll like it better than baseball camp, is all. 'Cause this place is a home away from home where you can forget about all that painful stuff and just be yourself with the people who, like, truly get—or at least truly want to get—who you are."

"Huh. I guess I'd never thought of camp that way before. Maybe it won't be so bad. Now that I've met you and stuff."

Rick announced the next activity, but Slimey had no idea what he'd said. It could've been the egg toss, it could've been the shuttle run, it could've been anything, really. All Slimey could hear was her heartbeat, and all she saw was Bobby, chewing the inside of his cheek, blinking his brown-caramel eyes, and waiting patiently for her.

"I can . . . do you mind if I . . . ?" he asked softly, looking down.

"Sure," Slimey answered quickly. *Mind if you what?*

Bobby bent down and tied the shoelace on Slimey's left Chuck Taylor to the shoelace on his right Nike. He awkwardly showed her the crook of his elbow, and she slid her arm inside.

"On your mark, get set, go!" Rick bellowed.

The three-legged race began, and Bobby and Slimey weren't in the lead—they were taking their time—but anyone could see they were perfectly in sync.

WANTED: Boyfriends

"The fact that they're calling him Smelly is clearly a red flag," Missi announced.

Slimey rolled her eyes and climbed to the top bunk. The girls had been gossiping about this summer's "fresh meat" for twenty whole minutes, even though no one but Slimey had even talked to him. If his nickname was worthy of a red flag, then so was hers. Slimey plopped by Melman's side and let her legs dangle over the edge.

"I noticed he was dressed like a flag, too. An *American* one, not just a red one," Jenny joked.

Jamie cracked up so hard, she nearly choked. Melman gave Slimey a *The J squad is still annoying as ever* look and aimed her soccer ball to chuck at Jamie's head. Slimey laughed into Melman's sleeve to muffle the sound.

"Fivesies!" Jamie swooped up five jacks from the cabin floor. Her stringy hair hung over her face, and it was a wonder she could see the jacks at all.

"I have allergy meds if you're feeling the aftermath," Sophie offered Slimey, her eyes glued to her vampire book.

"I didn't smell anything," Slimey protested. "Except piña coladas."

"So, he's an alcoholic?" Jenny asked, smoothing her yellow bangs to the side of her forehead. "Like, it's not bad if he's tried alcohol, but if he needs it to have a good time at camp, then that's a problem."

Slimey answered Jenny with an exasperated sigh. She'd wanted to ask Melman what she thought of Bobby the whole walk back to Anita Hill, but Jenny hadn't let up.

"What if I need hamburgers to have a good time at camp?" Melman asked in all seriousness. "Slimes, feel my monster." Slimey felt Melman's six-pack of a stomach. It rumbled like crazy, even though Melman had just scarfed down a Milky Way at Canteen.

Jamie swooped up five more jacks. "Sixies!"

"I'm bored. Can you mess up already?" Jenny asked. "It's been, like, five minutes."

"She can't mess up now—she's almost at tensies!" Missi shrieked, pulling her chicken legs to her chest. "Go, Jamie, go! Before Sara calls Lights Out!"

"Ow! Missi, you're hurting our ears," Jenny complained. "Jamie, make her stop."

"But her cheering helps me."

"Missi, stop," Jenny reprimanded.

Melman raised the soccer ball over her head, now targeting Jenny, and Slimey playfully smacked it down to Melman's lap. She knew her best friend wasn't actually going to throw the ball at the J-squad, but still, it would have been awkward if they'd seen her aiming. Melman nodded with approval—she liked to see Slimey use her reflexes.

"Well, he sounds kinda weird-sauce," Missi warned Slimey, her eyes bulging.

"He's not weird-sauce. He's . . . nice." Slimey looked to Melman for backup, but she was busy tossing the soccer ball at the ceiling. Boy talk bored her.

"Omigod, do you like him?" Jenny asked.

"Omigod, yeah, Slimey, do you want to go out with him?" Jamie asked.

"Omigod, yeah . . . ," Missi followed awkwardly.

"What? I dunno. I mean, I just met him." Slimey's heart pounded just *thinking* about Bobby. But she wasn't about to tell Jenny that. Or her sidekicks.

Slimey thought back to their One Tree Hill summer, which had been Jenny-free. It was awesome. They'd had giant Uno tournaments, and during Rest Hour they'd put their heads on each other's tummies and played the laughing game. On the last night, they'd dreaded the thought of being apart so much, they'd all smushed into Melman's bed at Lights Out. Slimey squeezed her eyes shut for a quick second and wished the six of them could become more like the five of them had been three years ago.

Slimey opened her eyes to Missi pointing at her cat poster. "There is such a thing as love at first sight. Like me and Buttercup Whiskers III."

"Did you just compare Smelly to a cat?" Melman asked.

"He wishes."

"Well, if you don't like him, Slimey, then can Jamie ask him out?" Jenny asked.

Slimey's heart stopped. "I mean . . . ," she began.

"No one cares about any of this stuff but you, Jenny," Melman said, tossing her soccer ball from hand to hand.

Slimey chewed the inside of her cheek, a little embarrassed. She wished she didn't care—she'd never cared about this stuff any summer before—but she couldn't help it with Bobby.

Jenny plowed on. "Um, it's not every summer we get cute fresh meat in our age group, so I want to make sure." She smiled expectantly, like she was waiting for her cabinmates to applaud her for being so sensitive. "Plus, Jamie is *so pretty* and *so adorable* and would be *so good* as a girlfriend."

Slimey felt a kick of jealousy in her gut. She could tell that Melman was staring at her to share a *Can you believe the J squad?* smirk, but she thought it best to keep her eyes on Jenny. "Well, I mean, I don't think it's a good idea. He just got here, and he's going through a lot," she said, trying to sound casual. She slid down from the edge of Melman's top bunk to the floor.

"Going through a lot?" Jenny said. "If he's struggling with alcohol and other stuff, then, omigod, hot-sauce, Jamie. He needs you. You have to do it."

Slimey puffed out a breath in frustration, half wishing Melman *had* tossed the ball at their heads.

Jamie's face emerged from her hair. "But none of us have ever been with any of the Rolling Hills guys. You think I should be first? What if he says no?"

"He won't. We'll make a plan. Omigod, it'll be so much fun. He could be your Christopher."

"Christopher!" Jamie sighed dreamily. "Have you heard from him yet?"

"Omigod, yeah, he texted me before dinner." Jenny slid her cell phone out from her cubby. "Miss ya. Smiley face."

"Omigod, that is so cute-sauce. You are so lucky your mom let you bring your celly."

"I know!"

"Did someone say 'cell phone'?" Sara grumbled from her bed, out of sight.

Slimey watched as Jenny shoved the phone back into her cubby and stuck her left hand into Jamie's sock drawer. Sara pushed through the hanging beads that separated her Counselor Corner from the Camper Cabin and caught Jenny's fingers fumbling through the socks.

"Je-nny . . . ," she articulated, shoving her palm out expectantly.

Jenny grabbed hold of what was clearly a different cell phone and gave it over.

"I get fifty bucks for every one of these puppies I hand in to the Captain. So, I will find ALL of them. And I will read your texts over the PA and dramatize those emoticons so hard, you'll be wishing cell phones were never invented." She scanned the room. "Anyone else?" In the silence, Slimey watched Jenny pretend to sulk. "Lights Out in ten." Sara stormed back to the Counselor Corner, shoving in the earbuds that were hanging around her neck. Jenny un-sulked.

"What's up her butt?" Melman muttered.

"You wanna know?" Missi asked, the excitement hissing out of the gap between her two front teeth.

"What's up her butt? Ew, no." Jamie giggled.

Missi darted her eyes around to capture her audience. "Sara's just mad because she only came back for Todd Bergman, who was supposed to come back, but then he dumped her AND didn't come back."

"They didn't break up!" Jenny snapped at her. "Why would you say that?"

"My sister told me, you know, 'cause she and Todd's sister are totally BFFs. Anyway, it's . . . complicated." Missi sighed theatrically.

Slimey peered in the direction of Sara's area. Sara had been so understanding and cool last summer when everything took a turn for the worse. She could tell it wasn't the right time to comfort her, but she wanted Sara to know she was there if Sara needed her. Not that Slimey knew what it felt like to be dumped. She imagined it hurt a lot, though. And she could relate to hurt.

Jenny collapsed dramatically onto her bed. "But Toddara is beautiful. They belong together!"

"'Toddara'?" Melman looked at her funny.

"Todd-Sara mash-up. Duh."

Missi squeezed next to Jenny on her bed. "OK, apparently he told the world he wasn't coming back to camp via Facebook status, broke up with Sara via emoji—"

"Which emoji? I know them all."

"Broken heart."

"Gross."

"Yeah, and he started hooking up with Jordana Tyne-Farnhorn."

"The lifeguard who saved my life?!?" Jamie asked.

"Jordana didn't save your life. She told you to stop breathing underwater," Sophie corrected.

"Well, if she didn't give me that advice, I probably would have drowned."

"Omigod, Jamie, I just want to put you in my pocket, you are so cute!" Jenny reached out for her, and Jamie clutched her finger the way a baby would. Missi reached out for Jamie, too, and Jamie clasped Missi's finger with her free hand.

Slimey had had enough of the J-squad for one day. She crawled into her bottom bunk and started to tape her pretty poster of melting crayons to the wall.

"Omigod, Jenny, I'm so sorry about your phone," Jamie said.

"Omigod, it's fine!!!" Jenny shouted loudly enough for Sara to hear. "I totally deserved it!!!!"

Slimey looked over her shoulder as Jenny slid her real phone out from her cubby. Jamie's jaw dropped. "I gave her my old one—hid it in your sock drawer," Jenny whispered.

"Omigod, you are a genius!" Jamie squealed.

"Shh!"

"You're a genius," she mouthed.

"It was my mom's idea. So, what should I say back to Christopher?"

"LOL?"

Jenny held Jamie's cheeks in her hands. "See? You're so good. This is why we need to get you a boyfriend, stat."

Slimey's heart raced as she finished taping her poster to the wall. She scooted back and noticed it was upside down, so she tried to peel it off. It ripped in two.

"I know, but I just don't like anyone right now."

"You just said you were totally into the new kid."

"I did?"

No, you didn't! Slimey wanted so badly to scream.

"Why are you blocking your emotions so early in the relationship?"

"I don't know . . . maybe I'm scared."

"There's no need to be scared. Having a boyfriend is amazing."

Ow! Slimey knocked her head on the underside of Melman's top bunk. A half-taped picture of a squawking Lois fell onto her comforter. She couldn't tell what hurt more—her head, or the idea of a puppeteered Jamie stealing her crush. She decided it was the latter. By a lot.

Melman's face appeared upside down over Slimey's bed. "You OK?"

"What? Oh. Yeah . . ."

"Can you imagine, Slimes, if we were like that?" she whispered.

Slimey shook her head. She could never imagine being as in-your-face about everything as the J-squad.

"What do we need guys for when we have each other?"

Oh. Slimey's heart somersaulted down to her belly. She

loved having Melman as her camp sister/soul sister/BFF, and she didn't *need* guys, sure, but . . . what if she wanted one?

Jamie's whining interrupted Slimey's train of worry. "I know, but Christopher's perfect, and what if no one's perfect for me?"

"What would be perfect is if you had a boyfriend. We could talk about them together! I'd be like, 'Christopher looks hot today,' and you'd be like, 'Yeah, my boyfriend looks hot today, too.'"

"That's a joke," Melman said, shoving her wild, dirty-blond hair into a ponytail. "Don't listen to Jenny, Jamie."

"WHAT?" Jenny lashed out.

"Just 'cause Jenny has Chris—"

"Christopher," Jenny corrected.

"—doesn't mean you also need a boyfriend."

"Uh, I never said she needs one, but, like, it would be so much better if she did."

Slimey pushed herself out from her bottom bunk. She knew Melman was fighting against boyfriends in general, but if joining her campaign meant getting Jenny off Jamie's back about Bobby, so be it. "I agree with Melman. I think you're having her go after a boyfriend for the wrong reasons."

"Why is it wrong to, like, want to be loved?" Jamie challenged Slimey, snuggling closer to Jenny.

"That's not at all . . ." Melman tugged at her hair. "What we're saying is . . ."

"Don't just want a boyfriend so you can talk about them together," Slimey explained.

"We'd double-date, too," Jenny added. "God, I'm the one with the boyfriend, people. I know what being in a relationship means. I'm not just guessing."

Slimey *was* guessing, but she'd bet all her lanyards that Jenny was wrong. "Still, it's more than that," she continued. "You should want a boyfriend you have stuff in common with, who you can, like, really talk to. About deep stuff."

"I don't have deep stuff," Jamie panicked. "Jenny, I don't have deep stuff!"

"Omigod, calm down. You have deep stuff," Jenny assured her.

"I think you're on to something, Slimes," Missi chimed in. "It would be amazing to have a boyfriend who also plays the flute."

Slimey thanked her with a smile.

"Or who's also a vampire," Sophie inserted.

Slimey cocked her head.

"We could harmonize!"

"And drink blood together!"

"You're not a vampire, Sophie," Jenny reminded her, "and also, ew, that's gross."

Jenny pulled Jamie to her lap and moved Jamie's mop of hair over to one shoulder. "So, what do you think, Jamie?" Jenny purred into her ear.

"About what?"

"A boyfriend!!!"

Jamie surveyed the room with her big, desperate eyes, and it took less than a second before everyone's opinions were un-leashed.

"You can survive without a guy," said Melman.

"You do know what Alexandria Millmont said about lovers when she was turned under the moon . . . ," said Sophie.

"If you get a boyfriend, I'll get a boyfriend," said Missi.

"You're not ready, Jamie. You haven't met the right person," said Slimey.

"The four of us can be a quad, Jamie!" Jenny yelled over her cabinmates. "Don't let them cloud your judgment. LET ME FIND YOU A BOYFRIEND!"

"Yeah, I get it, boyfriends are totally awesome." Sara whipped her beaded curtain aside, two marshmallows wedged into her mouth. "That is, until they tell you they're coming back to camp to be with you and then break your heart and stomp on it with their lies and perfect hair and strong calf muscles from running track!" She choked, spat the marshmallows out into the trash bin next to her, and started to sob.

"Are you OK?" Jenny asked, frozen with shock.

"I'm just choking on sugar!"

Slimey gently led Sara to the closest bunk, sat down next to her, and rubbed her back. "Hey, it's OK." She could tell things had just gotten a little weird, because their college-bound counselor was crying. But she knew from experience that anyone could break down, not just campers.

Jenny rushed to join them. "Do you wanna talk about it?" she asked. "Say all the good stuff you had together? Will that make you feel better?"

Sara nodded. Jenny smiled boastfully and looked at Jamie. "Listen up, Jamie. You're about to hear everything you're missing—all the perfection and popularity that comes with having a boyfriend."

Slimey looked back at Melman, and they both eyed the soccer ball on the floor and smirked. Too bad it was out of reach. Melman tapped her heart twice, and Slimey did the same before turning back to Sara. As Slimey listened to her counselor, amazing memories with Melman and the amazing memories she'd made today with Bobby floated through her mind like an end-of-camp slide show. *I could have a best friend* and *a crush,* she told herself. *Why not?* She pushed the J-squad drama aside and felt her whole body beam as she decided to make this summer nothing short of the best summer of her life.

June 30th

Dear Christopher,

How r u? I'm having an amazing time at camp.
I miss u. How's the lake? Did ur Dad let u
drive the Jet Ski? I hope so, cause that
would be cool!! I miss u. Do u miss me? Send
me a letter now please! I can't wait to read
it, cause ur the best boyfriend ever. It's like
I'm jealous of myself. Ha-ha-ha-ha-ha, LOL.

XOXO,
Jenny

CAMP ROCKS!

Date: June 30

Dear Uncle Frank, Aunt Gillian, Jess, Drew, and Sparky,

How are you? I am good.

Camp is ☺.

Today we ???? we woke up.

My favorite thing so far is Jenny

.

My cabin is wood.

The food is gross.

Write back soon!

From,
Jamie

July 1st

Dear Mom,

This summer the food is much worse than
last year. The fries are soggy and they
only have purple punch.

PLEASE, PLEASE, PLEASE with a cherry
on top can you FedEx me a package with:

    BBQ Pringles
    Honey Twist Pretzels
    Or stuff that's more healthy, like:
    Kudos Granola Bars
    3-Gallon Bag of Reese's
          Peanut Butter Cups

And normal stuff like:

    Gummy Bears
    Gummy Worms
    Sour Gummy Worms
    Funyuns
    Slim Jims

Oh, and a big turkey sandwich from
Dheli's Deli.

SEND SOON BEFORE I PASS OUT.

Thank you and love you,

Brian

Treading Lightly

Slimey held on to the edge of the pool to catch her breath, winded from a crazy-competitive game of Marco Polo with the Anita Hill girls. Now, with no one to chase after or swim away from, it was hard to keep her eyes off Bobby, who was struggling with the annual swim test. Next to Totle, who treaded water like Michael Phelps, Bobby looked like he was drowning.

Ever since their first coed Evening Activity together, she'd been itching to spend more time with Bobby, but they hadn't really had a second chance to connect. She'd even gone to softball for Electives, hoping he'd be there, too—but Totle said he was in the infirmary with a stomachache, which everyone knew was code for homesickness, especially when you were new.

"You got it, buddy! Ten more seconds!" Rick cheered, fist-pumping from beside the lifeguard chair.

Slimey noticed that Bobby's hair looked darker when it was wet, and it brought out a glint in his eye. It was a glint of panic, but, still, it was striking.

As Slimey practiced her underwater handstands, she reminded herself why Bobby was not on par with his cabinmates in the swimming department—he hadn't grown up here, and there probably weren't too many swim lessons at baseball camp. He'd learn soon enough. Slimey felt a tickle on the bottom of her foot. *Melman!* she thought. She flopped out of her handstand and popped up from the water, ready for a splash war. But it wasn't Melman. It was Bobby. Her heart nearly leapt out of her chest.

"I know it looked like I was drowning over there, but believe it or not, I passed."

Slimey giggled. "Well, congrats!"

"Thanks. I'm ready to start my Olympics training. I heard they're making doggie paddling an event."

She giggled some more. It was nice that Bobby could laugh at himself. "Actually, that's totally an event during the Rolling Hills Olympics. Not the real Olympics. In the Apache. It's the event after the Regatta before the Backwards-Alphabet Recitation."

He laughed. "Are you speaking gibberish right now to mess with me?"

Go easy. Bobby doesn't know camp-speak. "You'll get it. Happens at the end of the summer."

"If I make it that far. If things get sorted at home, I might not need to stay."

Bobby's words hit her like a punch to the heart. She wanted Bobby to be happy and for everything to work out with his family, but she didn't want him to leave. She felt a pang of guilt for being so selfish. "I thought you *wanted* to get away for the summer."

"Maybe, yeah, for a little while. But if things get better at home, then it could be nice to be there."

"Well, if it makes you feel any better, last summer Jamie's parents got divorced, and the year before that Missi's parents split up, and neither of them ever wanted to go home."

"Well, my parents are just on bad terms—they're not . . . I mean, they're not getting a divorce or anything. What about your parents? Are they together?"

The lump from the other day snuck back, and she swallowed it away. "My dad's—Yeah. They're—It's like . . ." Suddenly, she was lifted above the water by an unseen force. The next thing she knew, she was sitting on Melman's shoulders, gripping her head for support. She was glad for the interruption. It felt really natural to talk to Bobby about home stuff, but she was afraid if she opened up *too* much, he'd pity her, or, worse, all her feelings would explode uncontrollably, like a Mentos-infused Pepsi.

"Sorry, Smelly," Melman said. "Gotta steal this girl away. In case you two haven't noticed, everyone's out of the water."

Slimey smiled to herself as she noticed the empty pool. When she and Bobby were together, it was like they were the only two people in the world. She crashed into the water, adjusted her green Speedo, and tightened her ponytail. She caught Bobby staring, and it made her blush. Melman looked back and forth between them, arching her eyebrows.

"What?" Slimey asked.

"Oh, nothing . . . ," Melman said, smirking.

Slimey knew exactly what Melman meant. Bobby probably did, too. Still, the two of them treaded water in awkward silence, pretending to be completely oblivious.

They heard a whistle blow three times.

"Well, I guess that's my cue to get out," he said. "I don't want the lifeguard to retract her decision to pass me."

"Yeah, you'd look pretty weird in floaties," Slimey teased.

"Is that what they make you wear if you fail the swim test?"

Slimey smiled and shook her head. Somehow, his total naïveté about all things camp made her like him even more. She swam to the ladder and followed Melman out.

"So . . . are you gonna play Marco Polo with us tomorrow?" Melman asked Slimey, squeezing the water from her hair.

"Yeah, of course. Why wouldn't I?" Slimey said, grabbing her pink towel.

Melman shrugged. "'Cause it's girls only, and, I dunno, I just want to make sure you still want to hang out with us at swim."

Slimey squinted with confusion and followed Melman's gaze to Bobby as he pulled himself out of the water. *Oh*. As her heart pulled in two directions, she was reminded why she hadn't told Melman about her crush in the first place. She wanted to reassure Melman, but she also didn't want to make any promises she couldn't keep. "Oh. Um. Yeah, I'll hang out with everyone."

"Whatever, that's cool," Melman said, looking down at her flip-flops and then at their cabinmates leaving the pool area. "We should go, though . . ."

Slimey nodded. "See you later, Bobby," she called over her

shoulder, then raced after Melman and the other Anita Hill girls.

"See ya!" he shouted back.

Slimey noticed that he looked cuter than ever in his navy swim shorts, with his thick hair plastered to his face. He still had that glint in his eye, but something told her it was for a whole other reason.

Striking a Chord

Bobby lay awake on his bunk, gazing at the moonlit cobwebs hanging from the corners of the San Juan Hill Cabin ceiling. He'd almost dozed off listening to the hum of crickets and the steady flushing of the cabin's broken toilet, but that became impossible with the eruption of Play Dough's Darth Vader snores. He was relieved when Dover shoved a sock into Play Dough's mouth, but he coughed it out seconds later, and the snores had been unbearable ever since. Bobby tried to drown it out by listening to the Beatles through his headphones, but he only got through thirteen full songs and two minutes and three seconds of "Michelle" before the battery died.

He took a deep breath, and the smell of fart shot up his nostrils and into his throat. He gagged into his pillow. He wasn't sure who'd dealt it, but he suspected Dover, since he'd eaten three sloppy joes at dinner. The gas passed, and in its place, Bobby inhaled San Juan's normal stench of body odor and unlaundered socks. He checked his sports watch: 12:18 AM. Only two minutes had passed since the last time he'd checked.

Bobby had always had trouble falling asleep. The first time was after he'd played the murdered turkey in his first-grade production of *We Give Thanks*. Then it was other stuff that made him restless, like scary movies and nerves about saying something stupid in class. Now, if he wasn't being kept up by the cabin's jarring sounds and smells, he was worrying about what was going on at home while he was stuck here, barely adjusting to this weird place, too far away to help.

Bobby winced as his left foot fell asleep, the pins and needles spreading up his leg like an army of ants. He kicked it awake, and a random tennis ball flew from his blanket, over Steinberg. He shot up from his pillow with heart-pounding panic and cringed with every echoing bounce. "Sorry," he whispered to the center of San Juan, scanning the cabin for stirring bodies. He expected a pillow to be thrown at his head by Dover or at least an annoyed grumble from Totle.

"Don't make me eat the starfish," Bobby heard from below.

"What?" He leaned over the side of the bunk-bed, his head hovering upside down over a spazzing Wiener.

"Crackers and cheese, please, mouse-mouse," Wiener mumbled, his eyes sealed shut.

"Wiener, are you up?"

"Yeah."

"Me too. I can't fall asleep again. Wanna play cards or . . . ?"

"Yummy, Mommy."

"Wiener?"

Wiener smacked his lips together, exhaled a whistle from his nose, and lay still.

Bobby hauled himself up, collapsed back onto the thin mattress, and let out a sigh of frustration. Last night he'd counted

6,986 sheep before giving up. Listening to his iPod at night made him miss his dad (plus, the battery was the worst), and even though warm milk usually did the trick at home, there was no microwave here. He could still go with Play Dough's suggestion: leave a cup of milk in the sun and then save it for later, since it was hot in the cabin, anyway, but Rick said that would make him throw up.

Bobby heard a few faint strums of guitar coming from the San Juan Hill Cabin porch. He closed his eyes and tried to think of Rick's plucking as some kind of soothing lullaby. He gave it thirty seconds before a sudden charley horse in his left calf sent him shooting up in pain. He held his leg and let out a silent yelp. *That's it. I'm done*, he decided. He climbed down from his bunk and went past his sleeping cabinmates, right out the creaking front door.

Rick looked up from his playing. "Oh, hey, buddy. How's it going?"

"I can't sleep."

"Was I keeping you up?"

"No . . . it happens at home, too. It's a thing I have," he admitted, even though he'd promised himself he wouldn't mention Bizarro to anyone. *Get it together, Bobby.*

"Cool, cool."

How is it cool to have trouble falling asleep? Bobby wondered. His heart raced faster, and he found himself getting angry. Cool *and* anxious *are opposites by definition. I literally have to "play it cool" to hide my anxiety.*

Rick pulled the guitar strap over his head and put the instrument aside. "You try reading or writing a letter or something?"

"Well, you said lights out," Bobby said.

"Touché."

"And the flashlight I borrowed from Dover doesn't work."

"Why not?"

"He gave the batteries to Steinberg for some explosive science thing."

"Uh, that doesn't sound so safe . . ." Rick leaned toward the door, concerned.

"Can I just sit outside with you for a minute until I get tired?"

"You think I'm so boring, I'll put you to sleep?" he asked, smiling and bringing his hands to his knees.

"Oh, no, that's not what I meant. It's just, that's what my mom and dad—"

"It's cool," Rick laughed. "But if the Caperooski comes by, you gotta jet inside, OK?"

Bobby nodded. Rick grabbed his guitar, and Bobby took a seat next to him on the sports-equipment crate. He listened to Rick strum a few more chords, then felt the urge to make conversation. Rick was relatively normal, and it wasn't often that Bobby had him all to himself.

"Practicing for something?"

"Eh, just playin' around. You into music?"

"Yeah. I have three thousand songs on my iPod. Well, it's my dad's old one, but he gave it to me."

"Cool. What's your favorite band?"

"I don't know. The Beatles, I guess. Eric Clapton."

"I dig it—Clapton's the man. You a Phish fan?"

"My mom makes good tuna."

"You did not just say that."

I did not just say that, Bobby thought. *Play it cool.*

Rick slapped his guitar. "OK, baby steps. You know, if you're really into music, I bet with some practice you could be good at this."

"Like, good-good?"

"Yeah, like good-good."

"My dad used to play. He hasn't had time to teach me, since he works all the time, and I practice my pitch a lot."

"So, you sing?"

"No, like baseball pitch."

"Ah."

"But I guess I can sing a little. I'm in my school chorus." Bobby decided not to tell Rick he'd had a panic attack right before their winter concert when the male soloist was absent and Mrs. Levine was looking for anyone who could do falsetto. Unfortunately, Bobby could do falsetto. That's when he'd found the janitor's closet.

"Nice. I bet your dad would be psyched if you came home able to rock out on the guitar."

Bobby agreed. He and his dad used to hang out more. They'd make his dad's French toast specialty: fresh challah bread from the kosher bakery drenched in real eggs and butter and cinnamon, with powdered sugar sprinkled on top. But it had been a while since they'd done anything together. Maybe if he learned some guitar, they could play together at home. Or, if his parents went back on nonspeaking terms, guitar could be a good way to drown out their silence.

Rick handed Bobby his guitar. "I'm gonna teach you a chord."

Bobby held it the way he'd seen Rick hold it, and the way he'd seen his dad hold one in old pictures. He hoped he was doing it right.

"Ready?"

"I guess, sure."

"All right, here we go. You put this finger here on the top string, then this one a little farther down between the second and third fret. These here, on the neck, are called frets." Rick pointed to the metal strips that ran across the width of the neck part. "And then, the ring finger goes down here on the bottom string."

Bobby put his fingers in place.

"Good?"

Bobby nodded.

"OK, now strum."

Bobby ran his thumb along the strings. *I actually sound pretty good!*

"And that, my friend, is a G chord."

Bobby strummed a few more times. "You think maybe you can teach me more?"

"Absolutely. How 'bout during Rest Hours or something?"

"Yeah, that's a good time." Rest Hour was the time Bobby thought about his dad the most, anyway, since there was nothing to do but write home or watch Steinberg experiment with electricity.

"Hey, I've got an idea. How about I teach you to play a song for Campstock?"

"I don't know what that is . . ."

"Campstock. The talent show."

"Oh. Is it soon?" Bobby could feel his heartbeat accelerate.

"You'll have lots of time to practice—no worries."

"Right, but what if—I'm not saying I'll have stage fright, or—But what if—"

"Relax!"

Oh, sure, I can relax—no problem, Bobby thought. *It's not like I have an evil doppelgänger out to kill me.*

"Look, at least give it a try," Rick said, laying a friendly hand on his shoulder. "That's what camp's all about."

Bobby's mind raced. He couldn't perform in front of the whole camp! One: he didn't like being in the spotlight. Two: he didn't like trying new things in front of people. Three: especially new people he barely knew. Plus, Rick saw what he'd done on the first day. Did Rick want him to have a panic attack onstage? Yank down the curtain, wrap himself in it, and drift off to la-la land? Did he?

"Look, I'll be by your side. I promise. And this could be good for you. Loosen you up a bit, get you to start acting like a ballin' Rolling Hiller. Can't be a real camper till you've done Campstock."

Who says I want to be a real camper? Bobby thought. But then he remembered what Slimey had said about how camp was where you could leave your old problems behind and start fresh. He wondered if performing at Campstock would help him do that.

Rick grinned at him, all pumped. "So, what do you think?"

"OK." *Wait . . .*

"Yeah?"

No. "I'll do it." *You're an idiot, Bobby.*

"Yes! Awesome, dude!"

WHAT IS HAPPENING? Bobby could feel a rock sink to the pit of his stomach, bits of his life flashing before his eyes. He couldn't believe what he'd just gotten himself into.

"You OK?" Rick asked. Bobby nodded. "You know, these guys are pretty cool once you get to know 'em."

"Oh. Yeah, I know." *Have I been that obvious? I'm such a jerk.*

"And on that note . . ." Rick cocked his head toward the cabin.

"Yeah, I'm tired now." That wasn't a lie. Bobby had completely exhausted himself with worry.

"You're gonna be great, buddy—I promise. We'll start practicing tomorrow. Cool?"

"Yeah, cool. Thanks, Rick."

Rick put his fist out for a pound. "The ladies are gonna go nuts for you—you'll see."

The ladies? Bobby wondered. *Do you mean the Anita Hill girls? Would Slimey like a guy who plays guitar? More than baseball?* He pounded Rick back, and Rick dipped under Bobby's fist with a peace sign.

"Snail!" Rick whooped. The peace sign looked like the snail's antennae, and Bobby's fist looked like its body. "'Night, buddy!"

Camp gets stranger by the second. "'Night." Bobby headed back into the cabin, tiptoed to his bunk-bed, and climbed up. He pulled his sheets up to his chin and stared at the ceiling.

He thought about how he might accidentally mix up all the notes. His voice could crack. He could freeze up. He could choke. He could drop the guitar. He could fall off the stage. And, worst of all: Bizarro Bobby could bring out his inner freak in front of the whole camp. But if by some miracle he didn't mess up, Slimey might think he was awesome-sauce, he might fit in as a "ballin' Rolling Hiller," and this summer could turn out only half as bad as his summers at baseball camp.

Bobby curled up on his side and faced out toward his cabinmates, who were all sleeping soundly. He could hear Rick strumming softly on the porch and Play Dough breathing heavily through fluttering lips. Almost in harmony.

He closed his eyes and drifted off to sleep imagining his dad playing guitar to his mom, except his dad was Bobby, and Slimey was his mom, and they were floating on a cloud right toward a bolt of lightning that was about to strike them, but Steinberg deterred it with his JanSport of batteries, Slimey slipped off the cloud, his cabinmates appeared and held him by his ankles as he saved Slimey from plummeting down into a giant duffel two hundred feet below, they all bounced on the cloud, which turned into a hill and back to a cloud as it floated all the way home above New Jersey, where everything had changed, and his mom and dad were cooking dinner together, Clark Kent was bow-wowing and dancing around them dressed like Superman, Bobby was singing the falsetto solo still high in the sky, and everyone was laughing and calling him cool because he didn't freak, he stayed calm, he didn't freak, he stayed calm, he didn't freak, he stayed calm, and it was all gonna be OK.

July 7th

Dear Mom,

How are you? Camp's amazing!!! It's still so hard for me to get up when reveille sounds. It's like I want to throw something at the speaker when I hear it go off, but that would require me being awake! Sara threatens me with a squirt gun, which usually does the trick to get me up and off to morning lineup. Once I'm up, I'm really good.

I'm starting some Arts & Crafts projects, which are going to be amazing, by the way.

The girls in my cabin are Melman (you know Melman!), Sophie (loves vampires), Missi (loves cats), Jenny and Jamie (the girls who are really clique-y and "omigod" each other a lot). My counselor is Sara again (duh, I said that in my first paragraph!), which is awesome. She seems upset and stuff about personal things, but I think she's getting over it with our help.

One last thing, because I have to go to basketball: I tell Melman everything, but I also have a new friend named Bobby, and we talk about a lot of stuff, too. He's cute :). I love and miss you, Mom. Love to you and Lois Lane. She eating her seeds?

Love,
Stephanie

July 9th

Dear Mom & Dad,

Camp isn't as awesome as baseball camp, but it's not as bad as I thought it would be before I left. I thought the guys in my bunk were weird when I first met them, since they have all these chants they do, but I think they just really like it here, so they sing about it a lot. It's kind of a cult. But whatever, you can't be mad at me for that, Mom, since you're the one who signed me up. Don't say Dad and I didn't warn you.

I'm learning guitar from my counselor, Rick. And I'm singing while I play, too. I've had six lessons with him during Rest Hour, and he says I'm getting better and better. Sometimes he lets me practice instead of doing boring activities.

I'm playing baseball twice a week here, which is cool, but it's not enough. I miss home. I hope you get everything worked out.

Tell Clark I say bow-wow.

Love,
Bobby

Battle of the Sexes

Dover chucked the volleyball over the net. Slimey sprinted toward it, stumbled over the laces of her Chucks, fell forward, and caught it with her fingertips.

"Slimes! Yes! Yes!" Melman dove to the grass by Slimey's side. "That's my girl!"

Dover made a disappointed fart sound. "Time-out, Rick! We need to re-strategize!" he called out. Rick dismissed this with a wave.

As Slimey jumped to her feet, she glanced over at Bobby, who was sitting alone under a tree, plucking his guitar. She hoped he'd seen her crazy awesome Newcomb play, but he seemed pretty focused on practicing. She tossed the ball to Missi, who threw it backward. It landed on Dover's shoulder, then bounced to the grass.

"That's an OUT!" Rick bellowed.

Melman, Missi, Sophie, and Slimey cheered, "Slide down and rotate! Our team is really great!" and threw two claps in at the end. Slimey rotated to the edge of the court. Jenny was only a step away, sitting on the sidelines with Jamie's head in her lap. They didn't seem to be watching the game. Slimey followed their gaze to . . . Bobby.

"Oh! Jamie, you should call him Bobert," Jenny advised. "It could be your thing!" Jamie shrugged in agreement.

Whatever, Slimey thought, pretending not to care. Jamie calling him "Bobert" would only work against her.

"Who should I get to do our dirty work?" Jenny said, braiding Jamie's hair from a side ponytail.

"I dunno, one of the guys?"

"Yeah, of course one of the guys, pumpkinhead! I mean, which one is popular enough to, like, have pull with Smelly Bobert?"

A ball thumped against Slimey's aching stomach, disrupting her eavesdropping. It spilled out of her arms, but Melman caught it before it reached the grass. "Thank you," Slimey whispered apologetically.

"Just . . . stay focused," Melman said.

Slimey wondered if Melman was listening to the J-squad, too, or had seen her looking over at Bobby, or if she'd noticed nothing but Slimey's mess-up. She hoped it was the last thing.

"Nice save, ladies!" Sara called.

Slimey stole one last tiny quick glance at Bobby. He was still plucking away. *Get your head in the game*, she told herself. She bounced her knees, got her hands ready, and challenged herself to ignore everything off the court for the next three points. But then the J-squad ran their mouths again.

"Play Dough? He might have pull with Smelly," said Jamie.

"Ugh. That's sad." Jenny scrunched her nose. "How is it possible that Play Dough is the most popular San Juan Hiller?"

She un-scrunched. "He must have an amazing personality underneath all that flab."

Jamie gave her a puzzled look. "Your personality is in your stomach?"

"Play Dough!" Jenny shouted from the sidelines. "Get out, I have to talk to you."

Sophie lobbed the ball over, and Play Dough caught it with one hand. "What? No way. Newcomb—Battle of the Sexes style—is a full-on *battle* against you *girls*, and I'm not getting out until we've kicked your butts." He threw the ball hard over the net, and Melman caught it like an Olympic Newcomber, then threw it to Steinberg.

"It's serious," Jenny whined, petting Jamie's face.

"Not more serious than this game! We're about to make camp history."

"Omigod, do you really think you're going to make camp history from throwing and catching? That's the dumbest thing I've ever heard. You need to get out."

"Never!" he grunted as the ball smacked the side of his head. "Ow!"

"Thanks, Melman!" the J-squad talk-sang.

"Yeah, yeah. I didn't do it for you."

"But the rules say no spiking!" Play Dough complained. "I'm staying in."

"Overruled," Rick called, winking at Sara and putting his palm up for a high five. She gave him an icy stare.

Slimey thought it was cool that Rick and Sara were working together, because they were the counselors who'd been at camp the longest, but so far they didn't seem to be making the best team. Sara was obviously going through a tough time, and maybe Rick just needed to give her some space.

Almost as if Rick could hear Slimey's thoughts, he left Sara alone. He walked over to Bobby, crouched beside him, and adjusted his fingers on the guitar.

"Jamie, you're back in," Sara called.

"No, thanks! I'm injured."

"Tight braces are not an injury." Sara waited a few seconds for Jamie to join the game, but when it was clear that Jamie wasn't moving, she sighed and let it go.

Play Dough shuffled over to the J-squad, chewing a piece of pancake that must've been hiding in his pocket.

Three taps into the mic over the loudspeaker halted the game.

TJ: Is it on? Hey, sweetie, is it on?

Captain: The button is green.

TJ: Who loves Camp Rolling Hills? I know I sure do. We've got fly-fishing, tuna noodle casserole . . . Who wants friendship? I've got three hundred! Friendships, that is. Moving on to the weather: Mr. Sun is really making his golden presence known. We can't possibly expect any campers to stay inside cleaning the cabin day after day when you're luring them with your dazzling rays of shine.

Captain: Actually, it's very important that the cabins are clean. Inspection is happening now while everyone wraps up Activity Period One.

TJ: Wrapido! Wrap it up!

Captain: And be sure to write a letter home during Rest Hour. Especially you, Robert Steinberg. Your mother has called me seven times this week, asking how you're doing.

"Really, Steinberg?" Rick threw his hands into the air and headed back to the court. "You're making me look bad."

Captain: Don't make me suspend San Juan Hill Cabin from the Midsummer Dance . . .

"Don't do this to us, Steinberg!" threatened Play Dough.

"Rick, that's not fair!" Wiener panicked.

"Get it done!" Dover demanded.

Captain: Because your mother, Robert Steinberg, is driving me bananas—

TJ: —are filled with potassium!

Captain: And other nutrients.

The camp directors signed off with an annoying squeal of feedback. The game resumed, and Slimey rotated out of turn, close to the sidelines again, to better hear the J-squad. She fell into her ready stance and kept her eyes on the court.

"Play Dough?" Jenny asked him.

"What?"

"So, does Smelly like Jamie?"

Slimey froze.

"Jenny!" Jamie yelped, her eyes bulging out of her face.

"Uh, I don't think so . . . ?"

Slimey felt a pinch of relief.

"Why not?" Jenny snapped.

"Look at him. He's sitting over there by himself. If he was interested, he'd stare at her and, like, touch her hair."

"Is that what you think flirting looks like?"

"No. I dunno."

Jenny huffed impatiently. "You need to ask him."

"Wait, but—but . . . ," Jamie stuttered.

"Omigod, Jamie, obviously he's not just gonna ask him, like, directly."

Play Dough cocked his chin. "So . . . how am I supposed to . . . ?"

"You just have to ask Smelly if he likes ANYONE. And if he's shy about it, be like, 'Jamie's hot,' so it's, like, in his subconscious when he dreams and stuff."

Jamie nodded. "Oh, yeah, I like that plan."

Miraculously, Sophie got out. "Play Dough, you're back in," Slimey called immediately, not even caring about losing a teammate. Anything was better than having to listen to more of the J-squad's schemes.

"Score-sauce!"

"Slimey!" the J-squad whined. "We weren't done talking to Play Dough!"

Slimey shrugged. Play Dough hustled back into the game.

Jenny plowed on. "I'm gonna find you later, Play Dough. OK? Play Dough, OK?"

"Yeah . . . OK."

"Good," Jenny said, leaning back on her forearms. "Love happens because of people like us."

Slimey rolled her eyes. After all, she and Bobby had a connection. Jamie and Bobby didn't. *That's obvious, right? Right?* A ball hit her thigh, interrupting her thoughts.

"Wiener with the fancy moves!" Wiener sang with a fist pump.

"Zip it," Melman said. "No one wants to hear your voice."

Slimey was out, but she didn't even mind. As she stepped off the court, she stole her billionth glance at Bobby, but his eyes were still on his guitar. She felt a little awkward just walking over to him with everyone watching, but she was determined to say hi before the bugle sounded and the boys and girls had to split up.

"What's up with Bobby?" she asked Play Dough, who was rubbing his hands in some courtside dirt like a gymnast would with chalk.

"You mean Smelly?" Play Dough asked.

"I mean Bobby."

"Why don't you girls just talk to him yourself if you're all so curious?" Play Dough said to the J-squad and Slimey, but mostly Slimey.

"Maybe I will," Slimey replied.

Play Dough stepped back into the game to serve. "Yeah, I'm sure you're just gonna—"

Slimey turned and started walking over toward Bobby.

"Oh. OK, good."

Slimey's heart raced with every step. As she reached the tree, Bobby turned to face her.

"Hey! How long have you been standing there?"

"Oh, you know, like, twenty minutes."

Bobby laughed. "Yeah, that's what I thought."

Slimey smiled with relief that her joke had landed. Her heart was still beating fast, but it was a little steadier now.

"Wanna try?" he asked, offering her his guitar.

"Um, sure." Slimey knelt down beside him. Bobby held down some strings and gave her the go-ahead with a nod. She ran her fingers along them.

"You should go pro," he joked. "World tour."

Slimey bashfully flicked some blades of grass into his lap. "Maybe I will. But you'd have to be my band aide."

"A Band-Aid, like when you scrape your knee?"

"No, like, you know, when bands have fans who stick by their side."

"Oh! Yeah. So . . . you want me to stick by your side?" Bobby asked in a way that was a little bit awkward, a lot a bit sweet.

"Slimes, you're back in!" Melman called. "Wiener can't catch!"

Wiener huffed in defense. "My gel gives me slippery fingers, if you must know," he said, running a hand through his hair.

"Win it without me!" Slimey shouted back to Melman, taking a leap of faith she'd understand. As much as she hoped the girls would win, her "hi" had turned into a flirty guitar lesson, and she had no interest in cutting it short.

"That is so unfair," Jenny complained. "We can't *all* sit out. Slimey doesn't even have braces!"

"Cool it, Jenny," Sara said. "We have to leave for soccer in a second, anyway."

"Final point, folks, *finale punto!*" Rick bellowed.

"Nooooooo!" the boys (minus Bobby) moaned.

As the last throws were thrown, Slimey strummed the guitar and could feel Bobby grinning at her. Her mind was miles from the game. All she could think about was the boy in front of her, and how, in a way, he was turning out to be her Band-Aid, after all. The knee-scrape kind. With every glimpse and every smile, she could feel herself healing back to her old self—the Slimey who was always happy, without a care in the world.

12 July

Dear Little Ealing Fireflies,

Whassup? I miss you girls, and I miss playing
football aka soccer with you! Is Coach making
you sprint and dribble laps around the park?
I made the soccer team here. I'm playing
Sweeper with the fourteen-and-up girls even
though I'm only twelve. First practice was
today, and I'm wearing our uniform just for fun.
Still haven't washed it, for good luck. Shhhh.
Don't tell my parents. Still working on my
British accent. I promise it'll get better!

Kick butt, always.

#24,
Melman

CAMP ROCKS!

7/13

Dear li'l bro,

Camp keeps getting better and better. To say I'm popular is an understatement. Everything I do becomes a tradition. Like, all my catchphrases make camp history. And even though I'm the youngest in my cabin, it's like I'm the oldest when we play sports. In table tennis, I bring out the ping in pong. That's just something the little kids say about me, cuz I'm their idol when it comes to athletics.

Catch you later, crocodile.

Your big bro,
Ernie

P.S. Melman is in love with me—it's so crazy.

July 15th

Dear Grandma,

Got your present. Got your dollar.
Thanks a lot! Tell Grandpa that
I'm sorry about his prostate.
Whatever that is.

  Big kitty-cat kisses to Happy,
Sleepy, Sneezy, Grumpy, Dopey,
Bashful, and Doc.

  Love,
  Missi

A Reason to Smile

Slimey was walking to Canteen with Melman and the rest of her cabinmates, when she spotted Bobby sitting alone on the bleachers of Baseball Field 2. The sun was setting behind him, casting a shadow at his feet.

"Go ahead without me," she told Melman, giving her hand a little squeeze.

"Where are you going, Slimes?"

"I left my Canteen Card on my bed," she lied, jogging a few feet back down the dirt road, past the J-squad, her locket thumping against her chest with every step. "I'll be right back!" Slimey felt guilty for not telling her best friend the truth, but she didn't want Melman to feel bad or act weird about her skipping out on a shared Twix bar to talk to a guy. Things were weird enough. She knew it wasn't Melman's fault that she didn't understand her the way Bobby might when it came to family stuff. Melman's family was perfect.

Slimey kept jogging until her cabinmates were out of sight, then turned and headed back toward Bobby. He was listening to that same big iPod he'd been listening to on the bus, his head down in his lap.

"Hey," she called. He didn't answer. She took a step closer to the bleachers and tried again. "Hey." Still nothing. "Bobby, hey!" She waved a hand near his face.

He moved his headphones from his ears to his neck and looked up at her with swollen eyes.

"Hey, why aren't you at Canteen?" she asked as gently as she could.

"Don't feel like it."

"Not hungry?"

"It's not that. It's just—"

"You're not feeling up to it?"

"Yeah." Bobby attempted a smile, but it just made him look sadder. He stood up on the second bleacher bench and extended his hand out to her. Slimey grabbed it, and he pulled her up by his side. "It's good you're here. I can't hide forever."

His skin felt warm against hers, and she wished she didn't have to let go. It was just his hand, but, still, the contact made her stomach flip. As they sat, and the hyper butterflies subsided to normal butterflies, Slimey noticed a folded piece of paper fall out of his pocket and land by her feet. She picked it up and handed it to him. "Here."

Bobby looked at it, his eyes glassy and tired. "Got that this afternoon," he said, not taking it back. "Wanna read something messed up?"

"Uh, sure, if you want me to."

Bobby nodded slightly, then tilted his face away. Slimey cautiously unfolded the paper, a little afraid of what she was about to read.

Dear Robert,

Your mom tells me camp is good. This is a summer of transition, and it's nice you've made friends while everything at home is getting sorted out. You can write me at my new address:

46 Washington Street
Hoboken, NJ 07030

Random fact: The first officially recorded game of baseball took place in Hoboken in 1846. Write Soon.

Love,
Dad

Slimey looked up at Bobby. His head was lowered, and he was methodically picking dirt off his iPod. "I'm sorry."

He shifted his body so his knees knocked hers. "How could he just move out without telling me? Without asking me, or at least warning me, you know?"

"Yeah."

"I'm gonna kill him. I swear I will."

The butterflies in Slimey's stomach went paralyzed, mid-flutter. "Don't say that."

"Why not?"

"Because you don't mean it. Trust me."

"This means they're not just having trouble like they said.

They're separating or getting a divorce or whatever. And now what? I have to live alone with my mom? Or live part-time in Hoboken? I thought the whole point of me going away was so they could fix stuff—make it better between them. Not end it."

"I get that you're hurt, Bobby, but . . . Hoboken sounds nice, with the baseball thing and all."

He looked at Slimey and shook his head ever so slightly. "I know you're just trying to help, but there's no bright side to divorce."

"Not if you don't look for it. Some things aren't meant to make you happy, but that doesn't mean you can't try to find a little happiness in them."

Bobby waited a beat, looking deep into her eyes. "Can I ask you something?"

"Yeah, sure."

"Why are you so happy?"

"I love it here."

"And at home?"

"Home's fine."

"So, then, it's easy for you to look on the bright side. 'Cause everything's bright in your world, and in my world it's not."

Slimey pressed the tucked locket against her chest and felt the cool silver against her skin. She knew this wasn't the time to bring up her stuff. This was about Bobby. "Not everything is bright for me."

"Like what?"

"I dunno." She pressed harder, making the locket dent her chest. She didn't want to make Bobby feel bad by telling him the truth, but she also didn't want him to think she couldn't relate to his darkness because her life was so sunny and bright. She tried to think of a time when she'd viewed something not so good in a better light. Something substantial but not as substantial as her dad.

"Like, OK. So, last summer I was really excited for my parents to come up on Visiting Day. I spent all this time getting ready—put my lanyards out and finished up the rest of my Arts and Crafts projects so I could give them to my family as gifts."

"OK."

"And then it was Visiting Day morning, and Sophie and Missi and Jamie and Jenny and Melman all found their parents, but mine weren't there. And then Sara, who was also our counselor last year, found me and told me they were running late."

"How'd she know?"

"My mom called the office or something. So, anyway, I was really upset, but the Melmans took me in as part of their family, even though I'd only met them a few times. And they're really funny and fun so . . . yeah, I got to hang out with them. And it reminded me that you can find family here. They don't have to be related to you."

"That's one day, Slimey. This is the rest of my life."

And then, without thinking, Slimey blurted, "I know you're angry, but you should be glad you still have a dad!" She swallowed a lump of air and tried to calm down. *This is about helping Bobby, remember? Don't make this about you, and don't yell at him. Think of something cheery to say.* "You'll get twice the presents on Christmas, right?"

Embarrassed, she made herself look at Bobby. He was right there, his eyes concerned and gently focused on hers. "Did something happen to your dad?" he asked.

The damage was done. She knew she might as well spill the truth. "He passed away last summer."

"I didn't know. I'm sorry."

"It's OK." Slimey pulled her locket out from under her shirt. The moonlight made it glow like magic. "Even though I never told you, listening to you talk about your family made me feel like I was closer to talking about mine."

"It's good to talk about stuff."

"I guess, but talking to you about stuff without you, like, judging me or feeling bad for me—it was kind of nice for a while."

"I like talking to you for *you*, Slimey."

She smiled as best as she could. "Thanks." She squeezed her locket in her hand.

"That's pretty."

"It's from him. Right before he passed."

"How come I've never seen it before?"

"I'm not allowed to wear it when we play sports. And at Canteen and stuff I keep it tucked under my shirt, close to my heart."

"Maybe you should leave it untucked so other people can see it, too."

"Maybe."

"You know, I can't believe I'm saying this, but . . ." Bobby took a breath. "It's OK to be sad once in a while."

"I am sad once in a while. I just try not to show it."

"I don't like people seeing me upset, either. Trust me, when I'm in a bad place, I do some pretty weird things." Bobby patted the bleachers. "I hide. Literally." He tugged adorably at his hair. "But since I'm terrible at hiding how I feel, you can always show your sadness to me. It'll make me feel less weird."

Slimey let a tear slide out from the corner of her eye, then laughed as she wiped it away. "It's good to be weird!" Bobby laughed quietly and wiped another tear from her face. She'd done it. She'd let her true feelings out and wasn't craving fifty fleece blankets to curl up under. She didn't feel the full heartache of Pop Rocks and Sprite, either. She felt lighter, like the weight of some of those *I feel bad for you* smiles and awkward pats had been lifted from her shoulders.

"You won't tell anyone about my parents, right?" Bobby asked.

"Of course not. Your secret is safe with me." Slimey ran two fingers along her lips as if zipping them, then twisted the imaginary key. They sat in comfortable silence for five seconds before Bobby leaned in close.

"Hey, come on, let's race to Canteen," he said, nudging her playfully. "Whoever wins has to buy the other a Butterfinger."

"Let's make it two." Slimey smirked, and he smiled a big smile back.

"You're on!"

They raced up the dirt road, and Slimey felt the way she imagined Steinberg did when he played sports: short of breath, heart pounding, nervous, and exhilarated. She wanted to get a puff from his inhaler or a jab from Sophie's EpiPen, but she also wanted to ride this feeling for as long as she could.

July 18th

Dear Dad,

I guess since you don't live at home anymore, you didn't read the letters I sent. Maybe Mom read them to you, but she probably didn't. I'm learning the guitar, since I like music, especially the songs on your iPod, and I'm getting good. My counselor, Rick, is teaching me. He's helping me write my own song. It's kind of for a girl. Her name is Slimey. She's cool. She's not slimy. Rick's lending me his guitar to practice on. Oh yeah, and I'm singing my song for Campstock. Campstock is the talent show. It happens a couple of days after the Midsummer Dance. I hit a home run yesterday and everyone cheered. It was a line drive just like the one I did at baseball camp last summer that you said would get me into All-Stars. I miss you, Dad.

Love,
Bobby

July 18th

Dear Mom,

Camp is good. Remember I told you I'm learning the guitar? Now I've had way more than ~~fifteen~~ lessons. Maybe twenty. My counselor, Rick, says I'm a really fast learner and that I have a natural talent for it, which is cool. He's the best counselor at Rolling Hills, and I'm not just saying that. Everyone knows. Today we're playing baseball again. I hit a home run yesterday and everyone cheered. It was a line drive that went through Play Dough's legs cause he was eating Pringles. Dover tried to throw it home, but his arm isn't as good as Totle's. Not his actual arm, but you know what I mean. I miss you, Mom.

Love,
Bobby

The Midsummer Dance

TJ [*amid piercing feedback*]: Captain, is there anything special happening tonight?

Captain [*whispering*]: One, two, three . . .

Captain / TJ: The Midsummer Dance!

Captain: While the girls get all dolled up . . .

TJ: The boys might shower.

Captain: Well, they have to shower. Boys, you have to shower.

TJ: Because tonight might be the night you dance with that special someone.

Captain: Are you asking me to dance, TJ?

TJ: In a respectful, assertive, yet unaggressive way.

Captain: Oh, well, that's just wonderful. I accept. And maybe you'll also be inclined to take me on a backstage tour after we've danced?

TJ: Sure.

Captain [*whispering*]: No, that's not allowed, remember?

TJ: No, I will not take you there! Because then I would . . .

Captain: Get held back from Canteen.

TJ: Eek, that's rough.

Captain: And, Campers, try to make note of at least three positive experiences tonight that you can include in a letter home tomorrow.

TJ: Your parents think we torture you.

Captain: Well, that's not—

[*The speaker goes off with a squeal.*]

"Yo. Smellsky!"

Bobby was just about to enter the Social Hall when Play Dough hustled to his side. He put his arm around Bobby's shoulders, squeezing him tighter than his bow tie. "I know someone who likes you."

"Cool. So do I."

"You do?"

"Yeah."

"OK. Good. That was easy."

Since he and Slimey had talked that night on the bleachers, Bobby couldn't stop thinking about her. And he thought—or at least he really hoped—that she couldn't stop thinking about him, too. It would make sense that she liked him, since they talked during coed Activity Periods and Canteen about everything from family to school to guitar playing to sketching to baseball to pets to funny memories.

Well, everything but his anxiety. It had eased up in the last week, and Bobby saw no point in throwing that wrench into their relationship now. She'd been amazing about his home stuff, but as his dad always said: a person can only handle so much baggage.

Play Dough nodded his head up and down to the music pumping from inside the Social Hall. Bobby motioned to the door. "You wanna head inside . . . ?"

"Are you gonna dance with her tonight?"

"Oh. I don't know. Maybe."

"You've got to, dude! This is your chance of the summer."

"How do you . . . ? Did she say something?"

Play Dough raised his eyebrows, grabbed Bobby's arm, and tried to drag him inside.

Bobby could feel the sweat start to bead on his upper lip. "Wait, wait! Does she want me to ask her to dance?" He was sure he and Slimey liked each other, but he wasn't sure if she just liked him as a friend. They talked about personal stuff but not romantic stuff like dancing.

Play Dough released Bobby's arm and looked him straight in the eye, man-to-man. "Trust me, you should ask her."

Bobby smoothed out his tucked-in shirt and patted his hair to make sure it was still stiff from Surf Hair. Even though he didn't know if he should trust Play Dough on this, he followed him through the door. Play Dough had that kind of effect on people.

The music was blasting, the bass of the techno vibrating through Bobby's entire body. The hall was dark except for flashing yellow, green, and red lights. A disco ball spun from the ceiling. The place smelled like wood and sweat and cologne and flowers. Bobby took a step back so he could breathe.

"Dude, you're not gonna find her from there," Play Dough insisted. Bobby tried to stay planted, but Play Dough pulled him into the thick of it, scanning the Social Hall for the Anita Hill girls. Bobby looked around, too, following his lead.

Steinberg was onstage, DJ-ing. TJ was in the middle of the Social Hall, recruiting campers to break-dance one at a time. The Captain was walking around, waving her hands over her head like she was dancing, even though she was obviously just supervising. Bobby was trying to take it all in, when a blast of dense gas suddenly poofed him in the face.

"Fog machine!" Steinberg shouted into the mic.

Bobby rolled up his sleeves. It was getting hotter by the second, and he was the only fool in khaki pants and a long-sleeved button-down. Every other guy was wearing khaki shorts and a short-sleeved polo, two things his mom had neglected to pack him. Bobby had put on the bow tie because it was always a hit at fancy family functions, but looking around, he saw that it was very out of place.

Play Dough pointed across the dance floor. "Oh! Oh! There!"

Bobby squinted through the fading fog to see the Anita Hill girls dancing in a circle around Sophie. He had a feeling she was attempting her own version of break dancing, though she was kind of just rolling on the floor and kicking her legs up like a dying cockroach. He shifted his focus to Slimey.

"See her?" Play Dough asked.

How could I not? Bobby thought. Her wavy brown hair, usually in a ponytail, was down—on one side tucked behind her ear, on the other held back by a silver clip. She was wearing a light blue dress with pink polka dots and a thin silver belt. She was . . . beautiful.

"See that look on her face?" Play Dough asked.

Slimey was smiling. A beautiful smile, her cheeks a little rosy, her lips shiny, probably from lip gloss. But Slimey smiled a lot. "You mean, her normal face?"

"Yeah, dude. She's waiting for you."

"But, how do you know?"

"I just do."

That wasn't a good enough answer for Bobby. Just because they were friends and he thought she liked him didn't mean she was ready to dance with him! He'd be gambling with social suicide, and he didn't normally gamble with anything.

"Relax. This'll take the edge off." Play Dough whipped out a package of Mentos he'd stored behind his ear and slid an orange one out into Bobby's hand. Bobby threw it back quickly, but not quickly enough to avoid the orange stain it left in the creases of his sweaty palm. "No, dude, that was for later. For backstage. For your breath!"

"We're not allowed back there, are we?"

"Back where?"

"Backstage."

"No. Why would I tell you to go backstage if it's allowed?"

"I'm not following . . ."

"Look, if you're gonna kiss her—"

"Kiss her?!?"

Bobby's heart started to constrict. As if dancing wasn't stressful enough, Play Dough wanted him to go in for his first kiss? Was he crazy?!? He didn't know about that stuff. It wasn't like he ever saw his parents kiss, and most of the kissing he'd seen was in action movies when the couple was scraped up and about to get shot by the bad guys.

"They're looking at us! Pretend we weren't talking about them!" Play Dough erupted into a running man dance move, then chest-bumped Bobby with such enthusiasm, Bobby was knocked to the floor. Play Dough dropped down beside him and whispered hoarsely, "It's only first base."

"Like in baseball?"

"Yeah, dude, just like baseball. But with a little tongue action."

"How do you know? Have you done it before?"

"Look, dude, I wish. If I had a girl who was into me, I'd do it faster than you could say, 'Chocolate peanut butter fudge cake.'"

"That's not very fast."

Play Dough peered upward toward the stage. "Dude-a-cris. It's almost time."

"I don't know. What if she says no? What if she isn't ready?" *What if I'm not ready?* he thought.

"She's ready. Listen, she wants to, and Jenny's acting all crazy about it going down just as we planned, so you gotta do it."

"What does Jenny have to do with it?"

"Everything. She made up The Plan."

"Oh. I don't know, Play Dough . . . ," Bobby said skeptically. He got on his feet and brushed off the confetti that had transferred from the floor to his pants. "I don't wanna get in trouble. You heard the Captain. No Canteen for the rest of the summer."

Out of nowhere, Dover charged over and threw a red piece of fabric onto Bobby's head. "Voilà!"

Play Dough laughed, working hard to push himself up from the floor. "Hah! Yes, Dover, that's what I call magic!"

"What is this?" Bobby asked, holding it up.

"Steinberg found it in the costume stock. I can dance with it like a matador—"

"You mean magician," said Play Dough.

"Nope, PD, I mean matador." Dover put his hand on Bobby's shoulder. "But since you got the bow-tie thing goin' on, and bow ties are bold, you deserve it."

"Thanks, I guess." Bobby didn't like to be bold, but he did like to look good. Especially if he was going to impress Slimey, who had never seen him dressed in anything other than sweaty athletic wear.

"No prob, Bob Smelly."

Play Dough waved his hands excitedly in front of his chest. "Whoa, whoa, whoa!"

"Are you OK?" Bobby asked, bracing himself for whatever Play Dough was about to peer-pressure him into next.

"This is how you won't get in trouble, dude! It's a disguise. Wear this magician cape—"

"Matador cape," Dover mumbled.

"—and no one will know who you are."

Bobby imagined kissing Slimey while dressed like a super-hero, and he couldn't tell if his heart's sudden rabbit-rate was from excitement or nerves. Probably both. "Are you sure?" Bobby asked, uncertainly tying the cape around his neck. He doubted this would help if he got caught, but Play Dough was growing on him, and if he was going to let him down tonight, it wasn't going to be over a costume. It was going to be about going backstage.

"We all have your back. Right, Dover?"

"Yes, sir. I provided a cape for Smelly's back."

"See? You've got to do it!"

"Go, Smelly!" Dover cheered. "Do whatever Play Dough wants you to do!"

"He wants me to go backstage," Bobby said, hoping Dover would agree with him that this was a terrible idea.

"Backstage?" Wiener interrupted, gliding right into their conversation. "You're gonna go backstage?"

"Yeah, you and me," Bobby said, trying to turn this all into a joke. "You ready?"

There was a short pause; then Play Dough slapped Bobby on the back, and he and Dover let out a raucous laugh. Bobby got why everyone ragged on Wiener. Not only did Wiener kind of like it, but it also made Bobby suddenly feel like he was on top of the world. Or at least on one of Camp's hills. Like he belonged here, after all.

"Yeah, yeah, very funny," Wiener said over their laughter.

Totle emerged from a crowd of older girls, leaning his elbow on Wiener's head. "What's 'Yeah, yeah, very funny'?"

"Smelly here, cracking us up." Play Dough gave Bobby a high five. "He's about to make it backstage."

Totle bowed to Bobby. "For it was not into my ear you whispered, but into my heart. It was not my lips you kissed, but my toes."

"Why would I kiss her toes?" Bobby asked.

"It's very dark back there. You might not be able to see."

"Totle!" Play Dough shouted. "We're trying to explain how much we WANT Smelly to go backstage."

"Oh. Yeah, dude. It's awesome."

"So you've gone backstage?"

"By myself, yeah."

Play Dough shook his head with frustration. "Look, if you do this, you will be THE MAN. No one in San Juan has gone to first base yet, and we need you to so we can grill you for advice when it's our turn."

"Yeah, it would be sick, dude," Totle said. "You do it, you tell me everything play-by-play, and I'll record it all in my journal."

Bobby didn't want to be the star of Totle's diary. Especially since Play Dough had been doing dramatic readings of it at night once Totle fell asleep.

Dover started to pace. "You're about to go down in history with generations of campers who have made out backstage. What a thrill. I wanna be in your shoes. Can I watch?"

Play Dough jumped in before Bobby could answer. "No! Stop creepifying this special moment for Smelly."

"I almost went backstage with Melman," Wiener bragged to Play Dough.

"No you didn't."

"I've dreamt about it."

Play Dough ignored him, turned to Bobby, and held his shoulders. "Listen, Smelly. You wanna be the most respected, heroic camper in all of Rolling Hills?"

Bobby thought about it. After finding out about his dad splitting, Bobby had done everything he could to follow Slimey's advice to leave his problems at home, look on the bright side, and be himself around his new camp family. Even though he'd thought at the time that Rick was just doing his counselor duty when he said the San Juan Hill guys were cool once you got to know them, it turned out that he was on to something. And now that Bobby had actually made new friends, he figured being the MOST ballin' Rolling Hiller would be nice. "I guess."

"'I guess'?" Play Dough asked, as if Bobby had poured salt into his picked knee scab.

"Yeah, I do."

"You do, what?"

"I want to be the most respected, heroic camper in all of Rolling Hills."

"Louder!"

"I want to be the most respected, heroic camper in all of Rolling Hills!"

"That's what I want to hear!" Play Dough held Bobby's arm up. "Isn't that right, guys? If you were Smelly, you would do it and do us proud?"

"Yes, sir!"

"So do it for me. Do it for you! Do it for San Juan Hill!!!"

The San Juan Hill boys let out a big cheer, and Bobby was in the hot spot. But for the first time ever, he didn't feel embarrassed or panicked or anxious at all. He was about to get everything he wanted: approval from his new friends, a cool reputation, and taking what he had with Slimey to the next level. His heart beat fast with anticipation, but it was a good beat, a beat that was in sync with the music. A beat that told him this summer was about to get awesome real fast. "OK. OK, yeah, I can do this!"

"Sauce!" Play Dough cheered. "Now, remember the signal?"

"You never told me the signal."

"When the slow song starts."

"OK."

"So, what's the signal?"

"When the slow song starts."

"You got it. All right, here we go. Stay with me." Play Dough pushed his way through the packed crowd of twisting and jumping and clapping and hand-waving campers, closer to the Anita Hill girls, a few feet from the stage.

Bobby followed, stealthily dodging Hula-Hoops, glow sticks, and punch spillage. He checked himself for sweat stains. Present. He pretended to fix the cape, but really he just pinched his shirt under the armpits to give them some air.

Play Dough caught him. "Dude, let it go."

Bobby put his hands down by his sides.

"Now, dance normal." Play Dough bopped his head in all directions and raised his eyebrows at Jenny a few feet away. She mouthed something at him—Bobby didn't know what—then twisted and turned with Jamie in her grasp.

Bobby swayed nervously, then settled on a step-touch move with a few snaps. The snaps were dumb. He turned his hands to karate fists and twisted his torso. He stopped that, too, and nodded his head the way Play Dough was doing, plus bounced his knees. He was close enough to Slimey to say hi but far enough away to pretend he hadn't seen her yet.

Play Dough stepped close to him. "Don't stop what you're doing, dude. I'm gonna make sure the music's set."

"OK," Bobby said, continuing his head nods.

Play Dough brushed past him and lifted himself onto the stage belly-first, kicking his legs hard for momentum. He whispered into Steinberg's ear, and Steinberg nodded and looked out into the crowd.

Bobby averted his eyes, not wanting to call even more attention to himself and what he was about to do. He looked down and noticed Slimey's silver flats. They sparkled. Bobby inched closer and closer until he was near enough to smell her perfume. It was peach and rose petals. He waved, since he was too close to pretend he didn't see her anymore, and he definitely didn't want her to think he was being a jerk by avoiding her, but she seemed preoccupied with Melman.

"I can't believe you wore shorts to the Midsummer Dance," Slimey yelled over the music.

"What? I left my hat in the bunk. You're saying I should have spent two hours getting ready, like the J-squad?"

"I'm saying, you didn't have to wear your soccer cleats."

"Why? They support my feet and elevate me, like, half an inch. I'm practically wearing heels."

"Don't you want the boys to ask you to dance?"

"Oh, don't worry, Slimes, one will."

Bobby followed Melman's gaze to Wiener, who was grinning stupidly at her, pointing to the dandelion he'd Scotch-taped to his shirt. The girls giggled. Melman shook her head. Bobby glanced at Slimey, arm in arm with Melman, glowing. She caught him looking at her, and before he could even give her the chance to say hi, he looked down, then back up to Play Dough and Steinberg onstage. Play Dough gave a thumbs-up. This was the moment.

"Slow song!" Steinberg and Play Dough sang-shouted together as the music shifted to a soft piano solo. The colored lights went dark, and only the disco ball remained. There was no fog, there was no screaming, there was no pumping and jumping and waving. To Bobby, it was just him and Slimey and no one else. His heart was pounding so hard, it felt like it was going to fall out of his chest. Time seemed to stand still as he clenched and unclenched his fists, then wiped his sweaty palms on his pants. He took a deep breath and exhaled.

"Hey, Melman, wanna dance?" he heard Wiener ask, trying to sound smooth.

"Why are you walking like that?"

"Oh, I didn't notice," he said, dropping the swagger.

Melman nudged Slimey. "See? All right, let's get this over with." She extended her arms out to Wiener.

He put his arms around her waist, and she collapsed hers on his shoulders. Wiener looked at Melman, towering at least six inches above him, and smiled the widest Bobby had ever seen him smile.

"You just can't wait to brag about this, can you?" she said.

"I don't need to brag. Everyone can see the magic that's happening here."

She slapped the side of his head playfully.

Bobby looked over at Slimey, who was twiddling her thumbs, her smile at Melman and Wiener fading with every second. He looked at Play Dough onstage, who was waving at him with great urgency. Bobby breathed in quick, sharp breaths. He just wanted to get this over with—rip it off like a Band-Aid. Then he could either go bury himself in his duffel again if she said no, or enjoy being the luckiest guy in the world if she said yes.

The first chorus was coming, and the clock was ticking. This song couldn't be more than three and a half minutes long, and he guessed a whole minute had already played, leaving him only two and a half minutes to complete the mission.

All he had to do was ask her. It was a simple question, really. *Will you ask me to dance? I mean, will I ask—? Will you dance with my body? I mean . . . ugh! Can you—? You look pretty tonight, Slimey. I mean, you always look pretty. Wanna dance? I've got moves. I've got—No! I have no moves. I don't move. I'll sway. Please. Just dance with me. I'm begging you, not begging you, but asking, please, will you do me the honor? What am I, British? Ahhh! Slimey, dance-dance?* Bobby was sure he was going to die.

He couldn't look in the direction of the stage, but even from the corner of his eye he could tell that Play Dough was gesturing at him like a madman. He couldn't believe how confident he'd been on the opposite side of the Social Hall. He had no idea what had happened since. *No more thinking*, he thought. *Do it. Do it. Do it!*

Bobby stepped toward Slimey, one foot in front of the other.

The next thing he saw was Jenny pushing Jamie in front of Slimey. Jamie struck a pose with her hands on her hips.

"What are you doing, Jamie?" Slimey asked.

"Phase Three. Omigod."

Bobby had no idea what was going on. He looked at Play Dough one last time. Play Dough pushed his palms out from his chest. *Does he want me to push her?* Bobby wondered. Maybe it was like a human obstacle course—he had to fight through the other girls to get to Slimey. Prove his . . . He didn't know.

Jamie blinked her eyes all weird and smiled at him. "Hello, Bobert."

Even though she was acting strange, and no one called him that unless they were making fun of him, Bobby didn't have time to defend himself, so he just smiled politely. "Excuse me," he said. Then he took a deep breath, pushed past Jamie, and let it out. "Hey, Slimey, do you wanna dance?"

"Of course I— Wait, whaaat?" Jamie squealed.

"Whaaat? No! PLAY DOUGH!!" Jenny yelled.

"Oops," Play Dough said, hauling himself offstage to meet them.

Jenny extended her arms to Jamie. "Are you OK?"

"Yeah . . . ," Jamie mumbled sadly, falling into Jenny's embrace.

"I'm gonna take care of this for you," Jenny assured her. "Chicks before boys!"

What happened? What did I do wrong? Is she going to say no?!?

"Sure, I'll dance with you," Slimey responded sweetly.

"Really?" He sighed with relief. "Cool!" *Best. Night. Ever.* Bobby stepped in close-ish, leaving about eight inches between them, and put his hands on her waist like he'd seen Wiener do with Melman. She put her hands on his shoulders. After a few seconds she put some weight on Bobby's left shoulder and then right. "I think we need to . . ."

"Oh! Yeah . . ." *Dance, Bobby*, he reminded himself. *You can't just stand there, staring at her.* He stepped to the left, then to the right, then to the left, then to the right. Got a good sway going. He decided Slimey looked even prettier up close. Her eyes had a shimmer to them, and her smile was shy. Bobby smiled back at her for the first time tonight, and her lips opened, exposing her teeth, which were adorably crooked, pre-braces. They moved together in sync, in perfect rhythm, even more perfect than during the three-legged race. They got a little closer with each sway. There was probably five inches between them now.

Bobby looked over at Play Dough, who was now on the dance floor, and gave him a reassuring nod that everything was great (it was more than great!), but Play Dough didn't seem to notice. His full attention was on Jenny, with her sharp gestures, violent head-shaking, and scary-sounding whispers. Play Dough mumbled some defensive apologies in return.

Bobby wondered what the problem was. After all, he was dancing with Slimey. Their plan was working! It crossed his mind that maybe they needed him to ask her backstage sooner than he thought. Perhaps that was why Jamie had just hurried to the side, sulking. Bobby thought she'd done a good job, too—

being the obstacle course or whatever. There was no reason for anyone to be upset!

"Are you OK?" Slimey asked.

"Oh. Yeah. You?"

"Yeah."

"Cool." Bobby half smiled. He thought about dipping her to really prove the point that he was fine and having an awesome time, but he didn't want to drop her—she'd never go backstage with him if that happened—so they continued swaying back and forth.

Slimey giggled. "Look at Rick!"

Bobby looked over his shoulder. Rick was circling Sara, dancing like a zombie robot. "Oh, yeah!"

Sara pushed Rick off and moved to a group of female counselors dancing together. "I wish she had someone special who could make her laugh," Slimey said.

"Uh . . . yeah, me, too." Bobby wondered if he made Slimey laugh and if he should try to make her laugh now.

"Sara was really upset at the beginning of the summer because her boyfriend dumped her, but now she's halfway back to her old self. She's, like, letting herself have fun with her friends even though she doesn't have a boyfriend."

"Oh. Nice." He wasn't sure why they were talking about their counselors.

"Sophie and Totle are dancing, too," Slimey said.

Bobby looked to his right at Sophie hugging Totle tightly as he tried to squirm out of her grip. It looked more like torture than dancing.

"Is he into vampires?" Slimey asked.

"What?"

"Totle."

"Um. He likes sports."

"Oh."

Now Bobby was confused about why Slimey was asking about Totle. Did she like him, too? Was she just dancing with him to find out if Totle liked her? Did Slimey like vampires? "I like vampires," he blurted out.

"You do?"

"Yeah." Bobby floundered for a topic to avoid getting caught in his stupid lie. "Oh, look at Dover and Missi!"

Dover shook his shoulders at Missi while she made cat noises.

Slimey laughed. "That's so funny! Missi can be really funny sometimes."

"Dover, too." Bobby chuckled, thinking about how many cabinmates they had left to talk about before they ran out of things to say. It wasn't that he and Slimey normally had trouble talking to each other, but it wasn't every day that he was this nervous. It was a miracle he was able to speak at all.

Bobby looked at Play Dough again. Now Jenny had her arms wrapped tightly around his neck. It looked really sweet, until Bobby realized she was just using the slow dance as a chance to keep angrily whispering into his ear. Play Dough gave Bobby a thumbs-up behind her back. *It must be time for the next step.* He looked at Slimey, her head cocked in Jamie's direction. She looked concerned. He'd better do this fast. "So, Slimey . . ."

"Is she OK, you think?"

"Um . . . yeah. She's fine. So, look, would you—?"

"She doesn't seem fine."

"Oh. Well, I guess."

"I should check on her."

"Oh. Wait! Slimey, would you like to, um, go backstage . . . ?"

"What?" She took her hands off Bobby's shoulders.

"Backstage. Would you like—?"

"I heard what you said. I'm just . . ." Slimey removed his hands from her waist.

"Oh."

"I don't know if I'm ready for . . . backstage. I mean, we're not even boyfriend and girlfriend yet."

"Well, OK." Bobby felt like an idiot. What had he been thinking? Did he really expect her to go backstage with him when they weren't even boyfriend and girlfriend? *Unless* . . . "Do you want to be boyfriend and girlfriend?" *No!* He was supposed to apologize, not ask her out! *Say you were kidding.* "Sorry, I was just—"

"Sure."

Sure? Sure! Yes! Ask her backstage! "Good. So, then, we can go backstage?"

"I dunno. That's a big step, don't you think?"

"But Play Dough said you wanted to." Bobby turned to Play Dough anxiously. "Right? You said we should go backstage?"

"Oh. Dude. Plan sort of . . . ," Play Dough sputtered.

"Bobby! Are you asking me, or are you asking Play Dough?"

"You, of course! It's just that I like you, Slimey, and—"

"I like you, too. But what's the rush?"

"Well, I think it's part of The Plan . . . and this is our chance of the summer."

"What plan?"

"Phase Three."

Slimey took a step back and put a hand out to keep him from getting any closer. "I'm not part of some plan, Bobby! If we like each other, it's between us, not Play Dough or anyone else. I'm not like that, and I thought you weren't, either!" Slimey stormed past him and grabbed Melman right from Wiener's grasp. "I should have listened to you, Melman—we don't need guys. And whoever said it was right. Smelly *is* a red flag!"

All the Anita Hill girls and the San Juan Hill guys looked Bobby's way.

Bobby's face turned beet red. "What's that supposed to mean?"

Without answering, Slimey speed-walked to the back of the Social Hall, dragging Melman with her. As they whispered, Melman tossed a glare or two at Bobby over her shoulder.

Bobby followed Slimey with his eyes until she was out of the Social Hall. He felt a stabbing pain in his heart.

Play Dough laid a heavy hand on Bobby's head and tousled his hair. "What happened? You were so close!"

The pain spread through Bobby's body like a virus, eating at his patience and feeding his anger. "What happened is, you ruined it! It was none of your business, and I should never have listened to you!"

Wiener shoved himself between Play Dough and Bobby.

"Thanks a lot, Smelly. The song's not even over, and Melman's gone!"

"Blame Play Dough. He's the one who pushed me to do it!"

"Not with Slimey."

"You gave me a thumbs-up!"

"'Cause I was dancing with Jenny!"

"Ugh, you guys are idiots!" Jenny screeched impatiently. She wobbled over in her high heels to Jamie. "I'm sorry, Jamie. Boys are dumb." She pulled her in for a hug. "Especially Smelly."

"What did I do?!?" Bobby spat, his temper rising.

"It would have worked if you'd just followed the plan with *Jamie*," Play Dough said. "She was game for backstage."

Bobby felt his eyes burn, his hands shake. Frustration and confusion and disappointment and embarrassment bubbled in his chest, boiled in his throat, then blew out of his mouth. "WHAT ARE YOU TALKING ABOUT? There WAS no plan with Jamie or Slimey or anyone else! I liked Slimey, she liked me, and then you jumped in with your stupid camp rules, like, 'This is your only chance. Be the most respected, heroic camper. Do it for San Juan,' and I did it because for once I was starting to feel like I belonged here and belonged with a girl I think is really cool! But you know what? I was wrong! You're all a bunch of weirdos, and I never wanted to be friends with you anyway!"

Out of words, he looked around. Everyone was staring at him, eyes and mouths wide.

Rick finally intervened. "All right, boys, that's enough for tonight. Back to the cabin."

"Girls, you too. Let's wrap it up," Sara said, pulling Sophie off Totle.

Rick put his hand on Bobby's shoulder and gave him a look of major disappointment. Wiener and Play Dough were complaining behind his back. The slow song was coming to an end, and Bobby knew he'd just lost everything: his new friends, his new girlfriend, his new summer, his new life.

He bolted out of the Social Hall and down the dirt road toward San Juan Hill Cabin. As the stupid red cape flapped in the wind, he thought about how he must look like Clark Kent—not his pup, but the real one—failing to transform into Superman. His battle with Bizarro Bobby had always been a tough one, but he had no idea that battling his everyday self would be worse. *I am my own Kryptonite,* he thought.

July 22nd

Dear Journal,

As you know, every summer I set a new value system for myself. This summer it's S.T.A.R.F.I.S.H.

S is for Sportsmanship.

T is for Tolerance.

A is for Appreciation.

R is for Respect.

F is for Friendship.

I is for Integrity.

S is for Sensitivity.

H is for Helpfulness.

Also, last week I learned to turn laundry into a sport. Standing in the bathroom, I shoot my dirty clothes like basketballs into the laundry bin. If I get it in, I wash it. If I miss, I have to keep wearing it. I didn't make an interference rule, and since Dover interfered all my shots, I've been wearing dirty laundry all week. I smell bad.

Later,

Totle

P.S. No backstage play-by-play. Smelly chickened out, so I don't get to spill the bean-deets. Next time there's French kissing in the dark, I'll be on it. You'll be the first to know.

July 23rd

Dear Georgina Whitefoot,

Wooooooooo! I can't believe I'm writing to you. That you're going to touch this paper I'm touching. I just finished reading <u>Howling at the Sun, Part II</u>, and I LOVED it! I have a lot of questions, though.

- Why do vampires sparkle in the sun?
- Would you suck blood from a human if you were a vampire?
- Are you a vampire?
- If so, who turned you?
- Do you really believe love can happen between a vampire and a human?
- When Avina turns her younger sister into a vampire, is it to seek revenge?
- Was I meant to cry when Thomasina got staked with a wooden stake?

Here's the deal:

I like this boy named Totle. I hoped he was a vampire. He's not. I hoped I was a vampire. I'm not. I don't even know if he likes vampires. My friend Slimey tried to find out for me. She said she found out he likes sports. BIG SURPRISE THERE. His body is perfect. Anyway, he says, like, really smart things, like philosophical quotes, and it's dreamy. I live my life by your books, so I need your advice. Should I bite his neck and see what happens?

Your BIGGEST fan,
Sophie Edgersteckin

July 23rd

Dear Cassie,

Mom and Dad said i have

to so im writing to you even

though your stupid.

Ben

Campstock

I finally made it backstage, Bobby thought to himself. He stumbled in the dark toward a wooden bench in the wings, where he'd officially be on deck for his Campstock performance.

It had been three whole days since everything had changed for the worse, but being back here was a fresh slap in the face. And to top it all off, if the residual pain from the Midsummer Dance didn't kill him, he was sure performing in front of the whole camp would. He hadn't practiced or slept well, and due to his mom's terrible packing, he was stuck wearing the same stupid, too-hot-for-summer outfit, minus the bow tie and, of course, the cape. *If only I hadn't learned the guitar,* he thought, *I'd be an anonymous face in the crowd right now instead of about to be the laughingstock for three hundred people.* He walked hard into something metal.

"Ow!" Bobby yelped, holding his left shin. *That's it, forget it.* If he couldn't see where he was going, he would just wait for Rick in the audience. He turned, took two steps in the direction he'd come from, then remembered that being backstage in the dark was better than where he'd been—pre-on-deck next to Jamie and Jenny, who had been placed—what do you know?—

right after him in the Campstock order. Sitting beside them had made him so uncomfortable, he'd started to hyperventilate. And then he'd nearly fainted onto Jamie's lap. He'd go for a second backstage bruise over joining the angry J-squad again.

"Right over here!" someone whispered. Bobby turned around and was blinded by a flashlight.

"I can't see when you're shining . . ."

"Oh, sorry, dude." A shadowy figure moved the flashlight to illuminate a bench. Bobby limped to it and took a seat. The light disappeared and reappeared, illuminating Steinberg's face. He had a mic'd headset on and was holding the flashlight below his chin. "You have forty-five seconds, Smelly. No pressure."

"Right. No pressure. Thanks." Bobby nervously dug his fingers into the underside of the bench, right into a semi-hard glob of gum. *Great.* He yanked his hand out and tried to soothe himself with Missi's flute music. He couldn't tell if she was any good—he had no idea what she was playing—but whatever she was doing sounded nice and devoid of squeaks. He couldn't see much of her from the wings except her frizzy strawberry hair through a crack in the curtain.

"Thirty seconds, dude," Steinberg whispered next to Bobby. "Are you sure you wanna go through with this?"

"Why wouldn't I?"

"You still look upset. Just surprised you wanna sing and stuff for you-know-who in front of the whole camp."

He didn't. He absolutely didn't wanna sing and stuff for you-know-who in front of the whole camp. What on earth was he doing?

Steinberg gave Bobby a send-off nod. "Be right back. Tear all your ligaments."

"What?"

"Break legs."

"Yeah . . . ," he croaked.

Rick had promised that performing would get Bobby back on his feet, but he knew Steinberg was right: now was not the time. There was no reason he should risk embarrassing himself in front of Slimey. Not while she still hated his guts. Proof: he'd offered her his Butterfinger at Canteen last night, and she'd turned the other way without a word, Melman glued to her side.

"Ten seconds!" Steinberg whispered as he passed Bobby, sneaking through the crack in the curtain.

As Bobby thought about what his next move would be, all he could hear in his head was his dad saying what he always said: "A commitment's a commitment." But then again, his dad wasn't here, and he hadn't exactly been much of a committer lately. If he could break a promise, so could Bobby.

Bobby felt a strong hand on his shoulder.

"Hey, buddy! You ready for this?"

He looked up at Rick, who was all relaxed and ready to perform, his guitar strapped to his shoulder. Bobby's chest started to tighten, and he could feel his clothes cling to his skin, slowly sucking the life out of him. He had the urge to scream, to hide under the bench, to run for his life, but it was almost as if he were paralyzed. Bizarro Bobby had taken control. The decision was his. Bobby inhaled a sharp breath and let it out before he could find his voice.

"I'm not doing it."

"What? Why not?"

"I'm not ready."

"No, man. We talked about this. All your hard work . . ."

"I can't."

"Come on, you've got those chords down!"

"I was doing it for Slimey, and now there's no point. She hates me."

Missi finished her performance, and the audience erupted with applause.

"Wow, that girl can toot her flute!" TJ exclaimed. "Big round of applause for Miss Missi Snyder the fluter!"

"It's flautist!" Wiener shouted from the audience. Anyone anywhere could recognize his cracking voice.

Steinberg popped back through the curtain, holding out a music stand. "Smelly, you need this?"

Rick looked at Bobby expectantly, probably hoping he'd change his mind.

TJ continued on the mic. "Our next act hails from San Juan Hill. Let's give it up for Robert Benjamin, with some help from his counselor, Rick!"

Bobby tried to think about the first chord of the song, the first lyric of the song, anything about the song, but his mind was blank. Even though he'd been hoping that performing would help win Slimey back the way his dad had won over his mom once upon a time, he now knew that was delusional. Bobby got panic attacks. His dad didn't.

"Smelly! Smelly! Smelly!" the camp cheered.

He couldn't feel his fingertips, and his left leg was shaking under his pants.

"Settle down, boys," the Captain said sternly from onstage. She waited for them to stop chanting. "Robert and Rick will now perform an original song."

"Which means we'll have difficulty singing along!" TJ rhymed into the mic, making it squeal, per usual.

Steinberg's eyes bulged as he impatiently wobbled the music stand. "Yo, what's happening?"

Bobby stared back at him, not sure how to break the news.

"Well, what's it gonna be?" Rick asked him one last time.

Bizarro held his body hostage. He shook his head. "I'm sorry."

"All right, then." Rick left Bobby in the wings and hurried past Steinberg through the curtain.

"Rick! Rick! Rick!" the entire camp cheered. To Bobby, it sounded two hundred times louder than when they'd cheered his dumb nickname.

"Actually, we're postponing. Sorry, TJ."

"Not a problem, Rick-the-Clickity-Click-Tick . . . Stick . . . what else rhymes with—?"

"TJ," the Captain cut in.

"We'll just plow forward then, with Anita Hill's very own Jenny Nolan and Jamie Nederbauer dancing the night away!"

Rick reemerged backstage. "Hey, let's go, buddy," he said, putting his hand back on Bobby's shoulder and guiding him toward the light. They went through the side door of the Social Hall and entered the audience just as Jenny and Jamie, dressed in matching sequined dance costumes, hopped onto the stage. The audience applauded in anticipation of whatever dance routine they were about to do. Bobby was already old news. Good, he figured. The sooner they forgot about his wuss-out, the better.

"Just take a seat in the front here for now," Rick said, his voice ringing with disappointment.

Bobby plopped down on the floor in front of the Bunker Hill Cabin boys and felt his manhood diminish by the second. Not only did he fail Slimey, fail Rick, and fail himself, but now he was hunched down at the feet of a bunch of eight-year-old campers who'd already performed without a care in the world.

Girly pop music started up, and Jenny and Jamie put their hands on their hips and wiggle-bounced. Jenny smiled with phony cheer while Jamie desperately tried to follow her best friend's lead.

Bobby's mind raced with reasons he liked Slimey and not Jamie. Slimey wasn't a follower. And she didn't dance weird. And she smelled really nice.

The music faded. TJ bellowed into the mic.

"All right, then, that's it for Campstock, Summer of—!"

"WAIT!!!" Play Dough stood up on a bench close-ish to the back of the audience. Bobby knew this was coming, but he wished it wasn't happening so soon after his pathetic fail of a performance. "The San Juan Hill Cabin has an act. Rick, wherever you are, can you help us out?"

Bobby and his cabinmates weren't on the best of terms, but still, he was sure they'd be looking for him any second now—he was the only San Juan Hill camper not approaching the stage for the prank they'd been planning for two weeks, ever since the coed Newcomb game. Bobby knew he'd better decide whether he was going to do it or not before they found him.

Rick waved his arms in the air from the Boys' Side of the Social Hall. "Sure! Whaddya need?"

Play Dough, Totle, Dover, and Wiener pushed their way to the front.

TJ stalled on the mic. "Well, isn't this exciting? A surprise performance from our San Juan Hill Cabin boys! I don't know 'bout you, but I'll never forget last summer's hypnosis act. Robert Steinberg hypnotized Play Dough to eat . . . to eat . . . Hey, Steinberg! What did you get Play Dough to eat?"

Steinberg popped out from behind the curtain. "A beetle and cheese sandwich."

"A beetle and cheese sandwich. Right!"

Bobby was in no mood to perform, but he thought he should probably do it anyway, since he'd practiced with the guys and had a pink miniskirt waiting for him backstage. *You can do it, Bobby*, he thought. *One group number's not gonna kill you.* He tried to stand, but Bizarro held him down. *Who am I kidding?* He'd nearly had a panic attack five minutes ago just sitting backstage. If he couldn't even perform his guitar solo, how was he supposed to make it in drag? Bobby needed to let them know he was out before they wasted any energy hunting him down or, even worse, called him up onstage.

Play Dough met Rick up front and whispered into his ear. Rick went to the piano, and the San Juan Hill boys jumped onstage. Steinberg set aside his headset and joined them. Bobby got on his knees and waved to let them know he was up front but wouldn't be joining. Dover waved back, but he seemed to be looking right past him at—Bobby turned around—the waving Bunker Hill campers. Mortified, he lowered his hand to his lap. *Are they not going to look for me?* he wondered. *Why aren't they looking for me?*

"So, Play Dough," TJ started, "what is it this time?"

"Just a little something we've been working on."

"Fantastic. You all set?"

"All set!" Play Dough said, grinning mischievously.

Bobby sank from his knees to a cross-legged position. He wondered whether the guys had forgotten about him or were excluding him on purpose. Just because he'd bailed on his guitar solo didn't mean he'd bail on them. Well, actually, it did. But that didn't mean they shouldn't have asked. He wished they'd asked.

Rick started playing the Camp Rolling Hills alma mater. The San Juan Hill guys sang along in a proper, four-part choral harmony.

"Camp Rolling Hills
Our home for e'er you'll be.
In the bosom of the valley
Sun shines over thee.
Camp Rolling Hills,
Firm our loyalty,
May our hearts be filled forever
With thy memory!"

Bobby was suddenly getting flashbacks to his first day, when his bunkmates had psychotically greeted him with this same alma mater. All Bobby had wanted to do in that moment was make them stop—they were being so weirdly spirited—but now he'd take an overenthusiastic welcome over this painful feeling of being left out. *But, whatever, they're gonna look stupid, anyway*, he thought. *And stupid doesn't make camp history.*

"And now, a remix! Hit it!" Play Dough shouted.

Rick upped the tempo and added a jazzy rhythm. The San Juan Hill boys formed a line. Wiener stepped up from the center, ripped open his Lacoste button-down shirt, snapped off his Adidas rip-away pants, and, just as planned, revealed a bright purple dress with a sash.

The audience hooted and hollered as, one by one, his cabinmates stripteased out of their normal clothes down to the baby blue, yellow polka-dotted, bright pink, and shiny green dresses they were wearing underneath. The camp was cheering louder than Bobby had ever heard them cheer before, as the guys formed a messy kick-line and swung their legs up high, exposing their boxers. *Really?* he thought. *This stupid stunt is working?* He looked over at Rick to see his reaction, since the guys hadn't told him *this* was coming, but Rick was so focused on the keys, he still hadn't noticed what was happening. On cue, the guys burst into their "revised" lyrics.

"Camp Rolling Hills,
In the bosom of your valley
There is milk for me . . ."

"Is that my—? Are those all my dresses?" Jenny called out angrily from the audience.

"Hey, Steinberg!" Melman shouted to the stage. "Jenny says keep the dress—it brings out your eyes!"

"Ew, no, I don't!"

The boys crescendoed to their grand finale.

"Camp Rolling Hills
Makes me have to sneeze.
May our butts be filled forever
With your stinky cheese!"

The crowd jumped to their feet in a standing ovation. The San Juan Hill boys (minus Bobby) had made camp history. As Play Dough had explained to them in the rehearsal process, as long as the whole camp freaked out and the revamped anthem was remembered for years to come, their work was done. Even though Bobby thought this plan was stupid from the start, he couldn't really be surprised that it had succeeded. If he'd learned anything in the last twenty-seven days, it was that everything was backward here when it came to what was cool. Bobby looked up at TJ on the side of the stage, clapping and cheering alongside the rest of the camp.

The Captain was paralyzed next to him, her mouth wide open. "That's enough, San Juan Hill boys. Please get down from the stage and return those dresses to whomever you borrowed them from."

"They stole them from me!" Jenny yelled from the audience.

"To whomever you *stole* them from!" the Captain corrected herself. "And I hope everyone knows what you just heard is NOT our alma mater. Never again should it be sung that way." She took a few sharp breaths. "Let's start the dismissal process. Bunker Hill Cabin and One Tree Hill Cabin, please stand up and exit the Social Hall. Now."

Bobby self-consciously rose with the eight-year-olds and followed his cross-dressing cabinmates down the center of the Social Hall to the back as they slapped the hands of cheering campers along the way. He tried to stay close behind them, but it was difficult to keep up when their three hundred fans were in the way.

Once Bobby finally reached the back doors, leaving the way Slimey had just three nights ago, he felt his heart break into a million pieces. He didn't think he could feel any worse than he had after the Midsummer Dance, but now he felt like a total outcast. If the guys were angry with him, he thought maybe he could make things right. But if they just didn't care, well, then he might as well cut his losses and hang low for the next twenty-five days. After all, no cabinmate of his had shown an inkling of concern since the dance, Slimey had yet to acknowledge his presence, and even his mom had refused to pick him up when he'd called home two nights ago.

"All relationships are hard," she'd said, right before his seven minutes were up. "If they want to make amends, then you can, too. But don't push it, Robert. Some friendships just aren't meant to be."

July 25th

Dear Grandpa,

Got your present. Got your twenty dollars. Thanks a lot! Tell Grandma that I'm sorry about her arthritis. Whatever that is.

Big kitty-cat kisses to Happy, Sleepy, Sneezy, Grumpy, Dopey, Bashful, and Doc.

Love,
Missi

CAMP ROCKS!

7/26

Dear li'l bro,

I once told you camp couldn't possibly get any better. I'm never wrong about anything, but I was wrong about that. It did get better. It got crazy hilarious. Ever dress in heels and a bra? I have. And I made camp history cuz of it. Borrow Mom's. She won't mind. Now I'm more popular than ever.

Catch you crooked, alligator.

Your big bro,
Ernie

P.S. Melman is so in love with me, she danced with me at the Midsummer Dance and complimented me on my swagger.
P.P.S. I'll teach you my swagger when I'm home.

July 26th

Dear Mom,

I really messed up this time.

Send my medicine please.

I'll explain later.

Love,
Bobby

Operation Scapegoat

"OK, boys. Cleanup time," Rick announced, entering the front door of San Juan Hill Cabin with three brooms, two dustpans, and a fistful of garbage bags.

"Noooooo!" the guys—except Bobby—groaned loudly from their beds. Bobby wasn't feeling included enough to groan with them.

Steinberg took a stand. "Look, Rick, living in our collective filth has been preparing our immune systems for the apocalypse or an outbreak of E. coli. We can't give up now. We'd all get sick."

"E. coli or no E. coli, it's the Captain's punishment."

"I don't get what the big deal is," Play Dough said.

Bobby rolled his eyes. He also didn't know why the Captain cared—her camp was already a freak show.

"The big deal is, you guys defiled the alma mater, which, as you know, is sacred here at camp, especially to Captain Conservative. Hands over the heart. No kick-line. No strip-teasing. No stinky-cheese references."

The guys broke into laughter. Bobby stayed quiet.

"I know, it's hilarious," Rick said sarcastically. "Grab a mop, take a broom, and nobody sits till we clean this room."

"C'mon, these items are my inspiration as much as they are my supplies," Steinberg pleaded, scanning the unsorted laundry, empty Cup o' Noodles, and Cheez Whiz graffiti. "Robots don't make themselves."

Play Dough nodded, lounging in a pile of mismatched socks. "How can we clean if we can't even see the floor?"

"Great question," Rick said, handing him a broom. "I leave you in charge to figure it out."

"Oh, come on!" Play Dough whined, throwing the broom halfway across the cabin.

Rick strolled to his nook, pushed aside the curtain, and collapsed on his hammock. Bobby was tempted to follow Rick to his nook, but he didn't want to make a scene. He'd just lie down and listen to his iPod while they cleaned.

Play Dough sighed. "Fine. Steinberg, where's that robot dust-sucker thing?"

"You mean the one you sat on?"

"Yeah."

"It broke."

"OK, well, Wiener, fold clothes from the floor. Smelly, kick everything else under the beds."

For a split second, Bobby thought Play Dough was joking. But there Play Dough was, staring at Bobby, waiting for him to do his dirty work. "No way."

"I can kick stuff under the beds," Dover volunteered, bicycling his legs in the air on his top bunk.

"Smelly, you can fold with me if you feel more comfortable with that task," Wiener offered with a cocky grin.

Bobby felt his face turn red, but it wasn't a symptom of panic. This time he was just ticked off. "No, I mean, I'm not cleaning. I didn't get in trouble."

"We all got in trouble," Play Dough explained irritably. "One of us goes down, we all go down. That's how it works at camp."

"Then how come Slimey's only mad at me? Is that also how it works at camp?"

"Are you seriously still mad over the dance?" Play Dough asked.

"Yeah, I am! Why would you even listen to Jenny? Who cares what she says!"

The guys laughed.

"You have no idea," Steinberg explained. "Play Dough has been obsessed with her blond hair and blue eyes and the general shape of her face since he was in Bunker Hill."

"Steinberg!" Play Dough cried sheepishly.

Bobby tried to wrap his head around the idea that Play Dough would throw him under the bus for a girl who didn't even seem to like him back.

"Whatever, Smelly dude," Dover said on his back, his legs now extended to the ceiling. "This isn't about girls. Maybe . . . you should have done Campstock with us."

Totle sat up from his bottom bunk. "Like, I get why you didn't play the guitar in your emotionally raw state, but what we did had nothing to do with her."

"They were Jenny's dresses, not Slimey's," Wiener pointed out.

"If I wasn't in the MOOD to play the GUITAR, why would I be in the MOOD to SING the alma mater in *ANYONE'S* dress in front of the ENTIRE CAMP?!" Bobby yelled.

"It wouldn't hurt you to show some spirit. You're part of this cabin, too," Play Dough said, handing Bobby a garbage bag.

Bobby smacked it to the floor. "Am I? I was sitting right up front, and you didn't even call me up."

"And whose fault is that?"

"Mine," Steinberg admitted. "I told the guys to leave you alone, since you were displaying all seven physical symptoms of a nervous breakdown."

"You can't just mope around crying all day," Play Dough continued.

"I don't cry."

"Yeah, you do," Play Dough insisted. He scrunched his nose for his *I'm making fun of you* voice. "I'm so sad. My dumb almost-girlfriend—"

"She's not dumb."

"—almost made out with me backstage, but this other girl liked me—"

"Jamie? That's impossible. We've never even talked."

"—and now they both don't like me. Wahhhh! Wahhhhh!"

"Shut up!"

"Who are you telling to shut up?" Play Dough growled, pushing Bobby two feet back.

"You! That's who I'm telling to shut up!" Bobby lunged forward, knocking Play Dough into a pile of dirty, damp towels.

"Ohhhhhh!" Dover cheered, his palms forming a megaphone

around his mouth. Steinberg gave him his laser-beam glare. He stopped.

Play Dough lifted himself up and took three deliberate steps toward Bobby.

Steinberg climbed down from his top bunk. "Come on, let it go, you guys."

Gladly, Bobby thought. These guys were jerks, and he didn't come all the way to Rolling Hills to be friends with a bunch of weirdos who didn't actually care about anyone but themselves. Bobby shouted up at Play Dough towering over him: "For the record, I don't want anything to do with San Juan Hill or anybody else!"

"'For the record'?" Play Dough jeered.

"Yes, got it. Writing it down," Totle said, holding up his open journal.

Steinberg jumped between them. "Quit fighting. You guys are friends."

"A true friend stabs you in the front," Totle quoted, then jotted it down.

Bobby nearly spat in Play Dough's face. "Since when are we true friends?"

"We're not!"

Bobby was surprised to feel his heart sink.

Rick emerged from his nook. "Hey, hey! What's this all about?"

"I pushed him, Rick, but I didn't stab him," Play Dough answered defensively.

"In the front *or* the back," Totle clarified.

"What is going on with you guys?"

Steinberg started pacing and mumbling to himself. "What is going on with us? One: we're falling apart. Two: we need to be reunited. Three: we need something to reunite us. Four: what could reunite us?"

"Uh, how you doin', man?" Rick asked Steinberg, concerned.

"Five: a scapegoat! Holy Dude-a-cris! I got it!" Six heads turned to face him. "Nothing is going on with *us*," Steinberg explained slowly. "The *girls* are the ones to blame . . . Without them, none of this would have happened!"

The guys' faces lit up as they soaked in his epiphany.

Bobby was skeptical.

"Yeah! Yeah, see, it's not our fault, Rick," Play Dough agreed.

"They're driving a wedge between us," Totle added.

"They're making us act crazy!" Wiener shouted in a whacked-out voice.

Steinberg looked at Play Dough. "Are you thinking what I'm thinking?"

"That there's double grilled cheese for lunch?"

"No! The girls should pay for this."

"Pay for what?" Bobby asked nervously.

"There's only one way we can bring this group back together again," Steinberg announced. They waited with anticipation as he stepped up onto the first rung of his bunk-bed ladder. "An all-out . . ." He took a step to the third rung. "Raid on . . ." Fifth rung. "ANITA HILL!"

"YEAH!!!" they screamed barbarically with fists pumping. "Raid! Raid! Raid! RAAAAAID!"

"Operation Scapegoat complete!" Steinberg shouted.

"YEAH!!!!!" they shouted back.

"What?! No, guys, come on," Rick said, trying to settle them down. "You know you're not allowed in the girls' cabin."

"Please. Look at us suffering. We need this, Rick. And we need it bad," Play Dough whimpered.

"What you don't know won't hurt you," quoted Totle.

"Yeah, like . . . like see no evil," Wiener said.

"Think back to when you were a camper," Steinberg said. "Think about those classic raids you went on. Don't deprive us of a treasured camp memory."

"OK, OK. Fine. We never had this conversation, and I was napping when you left the cabin."

"YEAH!" they cheered maniacally. "Raid! Raid! Raid! RAAAAAAAAID!!!"

Steinberg took the lead. "All right, gather round. War-council time."

There was so much happening at once, Bobby nearly forgot he was angry. Everyone seemed to have moved on from the fight, including Play Dough, but that was no real surprise. His ADHD never allowed him to stay focused on one thing for long. Bobby tried to keep up. "OK . . . but, guys, what is a raid, exactly?"

Dover eyed him like he was from Uranus.

"It's our chance for defense," Steinberg explained.

"DEFENSE!!!" they shouted in unison.

"What does that—?"

"Will you join our brigade?" Dover asked Bobby in his deep, soldier voice.

"I don't even know what a brigade is."

"Neither do I," Dover stated proudly.

"It's a military unit," Steinberg explained. "All right men, fall in." Totle rolled off of his bottom bunk with black smudges already under his eyes. "Prepare your stations. Dover: intelligence. What do you know?"

"On the outside, their cabin looks like ours. But inside, I'd guess it's cleaner."

"We'll see about that," Wiener said, gesturing to his perfectly folded cubbies.

"Time frame?" Steinberg asked.

"I say we go now!" Play Dough yelled, slamming his hand on the side of his top bunk. "Ow!" He might have been the cabin leader, but he was too impulsive to lead a raid.

"Can I get a reading on the girls' location?" Steinberg asked.

"Pool," Wiener responded instantly.

They all looked his way.

"What? I know their whole schedule."

"And what is our cover as we climb up Anita Hill?"

"A bear," pitched Wiener.

"No."

"A hike," Dover offered.

"Good."

"Wait!" Rick jumped in. "I'm throwing in one rule. No touching the counselor's things. Got it?"

"Check," Steinberg said. "Play Dough, what's the status on Weapon Number Two?"

"I think I have it in me."

"Good."

"OK, two rules," added Rick. "Keep it in the toilet."

"Yes, sir. OK, Wiener—toilet paper. Everywhere."

"On it."

"Totle—shaving cream. Everywhere."

"Not taking mine," Rick inserted.

"Understood. We'll take the girls'," Steinberg responded.

Totle clasped his fingers together evilly. "Destroy the enemy with their own weapon. I like it."

Bobby waited anxiously for his assignment. He hoped it was something dangerously awesome like shaving cream.

"And, Smelly . . . very important. You be the lookout."

"The lookout? You mean, I can't—?"

"Well, somebody has to stand guard in case the girls come back," Wiener explained.

"Why can't you do it?"

"Because. I'm in charge of toilet paper."

Bobby was surprised by how much he wanted Wiener's job. Or Totle's. Not Play Dough's, though. He wasn't good at doing his business on the spot.

"Can we trust you with this responsibility, Sergeant Smelly?" Dover asked.

"Congrats on the promotion!" Wiener said, offering his hand for a shake.

"Fine." Bobby limply shook Wiener's hand.

"Good. I'll get the blueprint," Dover said. He dropped down under Totle's bed, grabbed his left hiking boot, and slid a folded map out from inside it.

"Dude, we just decided on the raid," Play Dough said. "When did you make a blueprint?"

"Years ago." Dover unfolded an aerial sketch of Camp Rolling Hills with red footprint marks paving the way to various girl cabins. "I didn't know how old we'd be when we did this, so I prepared this map for any and all ages." He pointed to San Juan Hill Cabin. "This is the path we want, since it's daytime and Anita Hill's our target."

"Got it?" Steinberg asked the troops. They nodded. "Everybody get ready. Camouflage, hiking gear, Silly String, Number Two. Then, it's time." They huddled up without a word and put their hands in the center. "One, two, three . . ."

"SAUCE!"

Before Bobby knew what was happening, the overly enthusiastic soldiers were sprinting out of their cabin and heading toward the back of the Head Counselor's Office. Distance-wise, about four soccer fields and a volleyball court away. It was all he could do to keep up.

Steinberg pulled up last, his goggles up to his forehead. He took three puffs from his inhaler. The rest of the guys turned around to see the holdup. "What are we doing?" Steinberg blurted out in between wheezing breaths.

"Shh! You're gonna blow our cover," Play Dough whispered heavily.

"Dover! What happened to hiking?" Steinberg asked.

"We're raiding the girls."

"Yeah, I know that, but don't you think it looks suspicious that we're sneaking around? Didn't you suggest we'd head toward the woods, past Anita Hill Cabin, for a 'hike'?" Steinberg used air quotes.

"Right. Good thinking," Dover agreed.

Steinberg sighed. "Men, let's march in plain sight. Act normal." Wiener started whistling. "Stop. Normal people don't whistle. That's only in movies."

"What do you want me to do?" Wiener asked, totally stumped on how to behave like a human being.

"Just talk . . . or something."

Bobby wasn't as clueless as Wiener, but his heart was racing so fast, he was sure he was acting anything but normal, too. As if trespassing wasn't nerve-racking enough, Anita Hill Cabin was also in front of a forest clearing where there had been rumors of bear sightings.

The guys stepped out from behind the Head Counselor's Office and tried to act casual as they strolled toward their Target. It wasn't long before they naturally fell into formation. Steinberg and Dover led the way as Vanguard, Wiener and Bobby fell back as Rear Guard, Totle preached Carl von Clausewitz's philosophies on warfare, and Play Dough ate three Kudos granola bars for fiber.

As they approached Anita Hill Cabin, their backpacks filled with toilet paper and Silly String, and Play Dough's stomach filled with poop, Steinberg reviewed the plan with the troops.

"We'll breach when I send out the sign. Wiener, you'll do the TP. Play Dough, you'll do your thing in the toilet."

"And not anywhere else," Totle reminded him.

"Right. Dover, you'll firebomb Silly String while I pilfer the cubbies. Smelly, stand guard by the door. Just sound the alarm if you see them coming."

"OK." Now that he was actually here, Bobby was relieved he could see what the raid was all about without the pressure of having to do anything outside his comfort zone.

"Don't worry, guys. I'll steal their deodorant," Wiener offered out of nowhere.

"Ew. Doesn't that go in their armpits?" Play Dough asked, sniffing his own.

"Yeah, but it doesn't smell like how our armpits smell. It smells like heaven!"

Bobby examined Anita Hill Cabin. It had the same six wooden stairs leading to the same wooden porch with the same sports-equipment crate next to the same green hooks for wet towels and bathing suits. The door had the same green molding, and the roof had the same chipped burgundy paint. The only difference he saw was the lack of dirty towels, baseball mitts, hockey sticks, cereal boxes, and muddy cleats littering the porch floor. It looked immaculate.

Steinberg rested a hand on Bobby's shoulder. "It's like no one is making robots here at all." He seemed to be reading Bobby's thoughts—which, knowing him, wasn't that surprising.

Dover looked to their leader. "Lieutenant Steinberg?"

"Site clear." Steinberg held up a fist, slammed it to his side, and clicked his hiking boots together. "Ready . . . STRIKE!"

Bobby's heart went wild, like he was about to strike or get struck, not like he was about to look out on a bunch of peaceful, rolling hills.

Play Dough charged up the steps first, barged into Anita Hill Cabin, and stopped short. "Whoa," he whispered in awe.

"Move!" Wiener cried. "I wanna see!"

Play Dough stepped aside, and the boys scanned the neat clutter of female stuff. Walls: posters, pictures, chore wheel. Shelves: Arts & Crafts projects, journals, chapter books. Cubbies: bright clothes. Floor: rainbow rugs. Ceiling: cobweb-free.

"Lots of pink," Steinberg observed, then took a whiff. "It smells like Hawaii and strawberry and wood and trees. Plenty pleasant for pilfering."

Bobby sucked in some air to lower his heart rate, then peered over Steinberg's head to look for Slimey's bed. His eyes went straight to a top bunk with a soccer ball on the pillow and shin guards Velcro-ed around the ladder post. He assumed that was where Melman slept, which probably meant that the baby blue and yellow comforter below was Slimey's. It was simple and only sort of neatly tucked, and it was worn, like she'd been sleeping with it every summer. It wasn't what Bobby expected, but he didn't know what he'd expected. Maybe something more special, like she was. He suddenly spotted the locket dangling over her bed and felt a twinge of guilt for invading her privacy.

"Keep an eye out," Steinberg reminded Bobby, moving into the cabin. "It's pilfer time." It was the second time Steinberg had said *pilfer*, and Bobby still didn't know what it meant, but it didn't sound good. He was worried about Slimey's stuff. He couldn't neglect his responsibility as lookout, though. The guys would never forgive him if the girls caught them mid-attack.

Bobby stepped outside and looked down the hill. Nothing.

His heart was still racing, though—all the laughter and commotion from inside the cabin seemed to be echoing in the air, adding a level of danger to his job he wasn't prepared for. Now he thought he'd rather be with the group. He didn't want to vandalize the girls' cabin, but he also didn't want to be the first culprit spotted. Plus, Bobby didn't want to miss out on the fun. He turned back to the guys.

Steinberg put a sandal and a stuffed frog into his JanSport. (So *pilfering* meant stealing stuff, but so far that stuff wasn't Slimey's.) Totle shaving-creamed his initials onto a wall, then added a mustache to a cat poster. Wiener skipped around, hanging toilet paper so it draped like ribbon decorations from top bunk to top bunk. Dover released Silly String with no apparent strategy in place. Play Dough groaned loudly from the bathroom.

"I'm having a baby! I can feel it coming out!"

"Let me see!" Wiener shouted, tripping on Silly String on his way toward the bathroom.

"This is a six-pounder for sure!" Play Dough bragged. His record was two pounds, so the bragging was justified.

Totle shot Wiener with shaving cream. "Immediate family only."

"Oh, come on! Shaving cream stains, dude!"

The bugle blared through a speaker in the cabin, signaling the end of the Activity Period. Bobby's heart sped up, and he threw himself onto the porch to keep watch. A chipmunk scuttled past, and Bobby leapt onto the girls' sports-equipment crate. He really had to get a grip.

"The girls are leaving the pool!" Steinberg called out. He seemed more distant, like he was toward the back of the cabin. Near Slimey's bed. "I repeat, the girls are leaving the pool. Recalibrate under the time crunch."

Bobby jumped off the equipment crate and peeked through the door. This was not the time to break focus, but his worry about Slimey's stuff took over.

"Quickly!" Dover shouted, frantically spraying Silly String inside pillowcases.

Bobby watched Steinberg grab a pair of socks, a beanbag pillow, and a lanyard key chain from Slimey's bed. *At least he didn't take her locket.* Steinberg then headed toward the bunkbed in front of Dover. He yanked out a whole stack of T-shirts from an adjacent cubby and pulled a shiny yellow belt from a plastic hook on the wall. "Too much stealth can go under the radar," he explained, shoving everything into his JanSport. "At least now the girls'll know they've been pilfered."

Bobby cracked his knuckles, relieved that Steinberg's damage was done, and glanced back down the hill. His heart was beating out of his chest. He knew the girls would be coming any second now, but they weren't in sight just yet.

The guttural sounds of Dover's laughter broke Bobby's concentration. He turned around to see Wiener dressed in a soccer jersey and stomping around in red high heels. He posed dramatically, faced the wall, and groped the number 24 embroidered on the back. "I'm making out with Melman!" The guys exploded with laughter.

Steinberg checked his watch. "You're straying from your objective, Wiener. We have T-minus sixty seconds to retreat from the war zone. Stick to the toilet paper."

"Wiener made a tapestry of butt wipes, Steinberg! It's beautiful!" Dover exclaimed.

Totle farted loudly as he laughed on the floor, which really sent everyone over the edge.

Play Dough emerged from the bathroom and ran up and down the cabin slapping the guys' outstretched palms. "I birthed a killer whale from my anus! Didn't even wash my hands!"

"We have thirty seconds to deploy, guys!" Steinberg pleaded, rummaging through the plastic drawers next to Slimey's bed.

Bobby's heart sank. Hadn't Steinberg taken enough of her stuff? He had to act fast. "Alarm, alarm, alarm!" he yelled, flinging himself into the cabin.

Steinberg leapt back. Bobby scrambled to the porch, and, sure enough, Jenny and Jamie appeared in the distance, followed by the rest of the Anita Hill girls.

"Take it off, Wiener! We have to go!" Steinberg yelled wildly, moving his pointer finger in circles above his head. "Wrap it up! Men, fall out!"

The guys jogged through the back door, slapping each other high fives as they went.

Bobby followed, sweat dripping down the sides of his panicked face.

Steinberg waited for the rest to run off, then jogged beside Bobby. After a few synchronized paces, he said, "Hey, Smelly, in regard to Campstock . . ."

"What about it?"

"Would you have done the number with us? Had we called you up?"

Bobby jogged silently beside him for a few seconds. "Honestly? Probably not. I don't really do stuff like that."

"Why not?"

Bobby furrowed his brow. He didn't want to say it, but singing an ode to the camp in drag wouldn't have been the coolest of moves.

"Dude, you hid in your duffel the first day."

"So?" Bobby asked defensively. He'd hoped the guys had forgotten.

"Embrace your inner weirdness, Smelly. I'm telling you, we'll embrace it, too." Steinberg gave him a salute, and reluctantly Bobby saluted him back.

A few feet ahead, Play Dough jogged in place until Bobby caught up. "Well done, Sergeant Smelly," he said, patting Bobby on the back.

Bobby's lips turned up, forming an ever-so-slight smile. Maybe the brothers of San Juan were at long last united.

As they reached the woods behind Anita Hill Cabin, a domino effect of girly screams filled the Rolling Hills air. Steinberg took one more puff from his inhaler, pulled his tinted goggles down over his eyes, and gave Bobby a nod of approval. Bobby's heart swelled with pride for following through with Steinberg's Operation, and pride for his cabinmates for pulling it off without a snag. Forget bears. He wasn't scared of them. The San Juan Hill warriors were the only dangerous wildlife in sight.

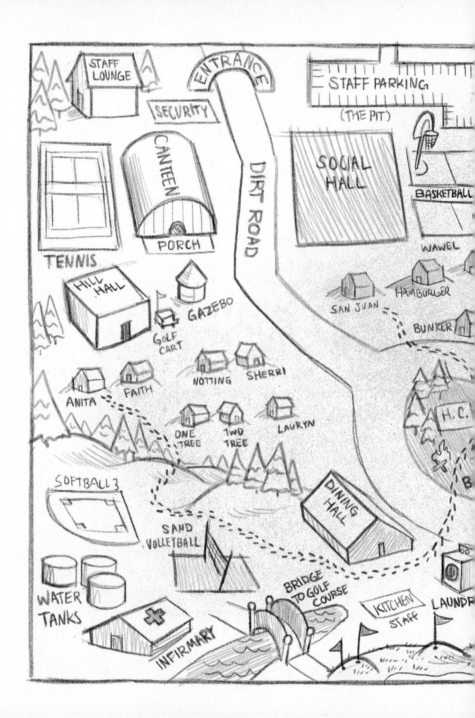

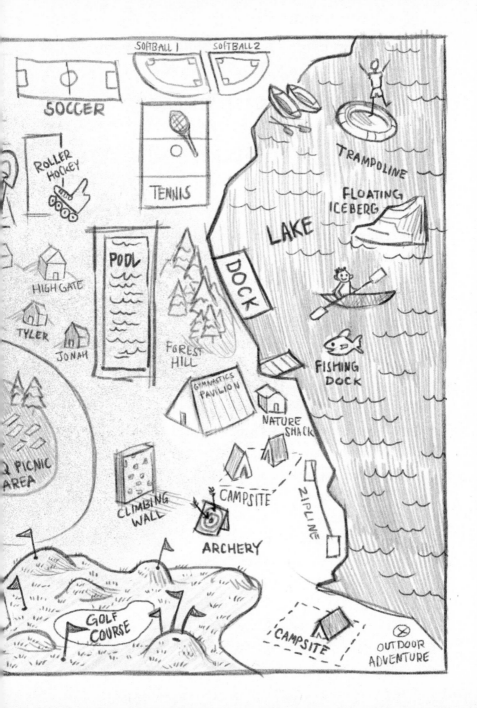

Hell Hath No Fury

Slimey was wrapped in a pool towel, hopping up the porch steps behind her cabinmates, when she heard it: Jenny's piercing scream, coming from inside.

Jamie was second to enter the cabin. "Jenny! What happened? Are you— Ahhhhhhh!"

Missi rushed after her. "Jamie, are you O—? My kitty poster! AHHHHHH!"

Slimey stumbled into Anita Hill right behind Missi to find their cabin in complete disarray. Silly String filled the place like colorful cobwebs in a haunted house, toilet paper draped the top bunks like a mummified fortress, shaving creamed *J.P.*'s marked the walls, and the place smelled like horse manure. "What-the-what happened here?" she mumbled, walking through the unnatural disaster with caution.

Jamie pointed to Missi's favorite cat poster. "Aw, is that a mustache?"

Missi mournfully tore it down. "R.I.P., Buttercup Whiskers III."

"Forget about your cat poster—what's that smell?" Sophie whined. "I can't breathe."

"Omigod, omigod, omigod!" Jenny cried in a nasal voice, pinching her nose.

Slimey followed the smell toward the bathroom, squishing Silly String beneath her pool-soaked flip-flops.

"Where's my yellow glow-in-the-dark belt?" Sophie asked frantically, ripping through her cubbies and then crawling under her bed.

"I'm missing shirts and shorts and stuff," Missi complained.

"How many?" Melman asked.

"Um, like five or twenty or something. I dunno—my cubby looks emptier."

"Uh-oh. Anyone else?" Melman asked.

Omigod, what about—? Slimey panicked as she met Melman by their bunk-bed and looked up quickly, expecting the worst. But there it was, all shiny, hanging from the underside of Melman's bunk.

"Don't worry, Slimes," Melman assured her. "That was the first thing I checked."

"You're the best," Slimey said, clutching her best friend's arm. She crossed her fingers that the rest of her belongings had been left alone. It took her less than two seconds to notice that her Mooshi pillow and lanyard key chain weren't where she'd left them. She tore her comforter off and looked underneath it. Nothing. *Why would anyone steal my pillow and lanyard?* she thought. She anxiously rummaged through the rest of her stuff. Sneakers: check. Sweatshirts: check. Socks: she wasn't sure how many she'd had before, but the quantity looked all right . . . check. Underwear: same. Check.

Slimey guessed everything else was there, just messier than she'd remembered. She slid open her bottom plastic drawer, where she kept her fancy stuff. Inside was coconut lip gloss, a pretty silver hair clip, a jean skirt, three cardigans, a small purse, five samples of perfume, two pink bandanas, and . . . *Where is it?*

"What are you missing, Slimes?" Melman asked. She always knew when something was up.

"My Midsummer Dance dress. I know it was in there."

Melman pulled out the whole drawer and dumped its contents onto Slimey's bed, sifting through them. "Yeah, it's definitely gone."

Slimey sort of understood someone quickly snatching the lanyard and pillow, since they were right on her bed—an easy grab. But her dress? She was sure someone must have *wanted* that dress. *Searched* for that dress. Deliberately *stolen* that dress. And in Slimey's mind that someone must've been the guy who'd wanted to go backstage with her in that dress.

"Do you think Bobby took it?" Slimey asked Melman, hoping she'd say no.

Melman shrugged. "I mean . . . ever since his foul play, he's been stalking you at Canteen. He clearly wants your attention."

Slimey knew that was sort of true—the attention part, at least—but she didn't expect he'd go this far to get it. But then again, how much did she even know about Bobby? She knew he was from New Jersey, she knew he liked baseball, she knew he was learning guitar, and she knew his parents were separated. But there was clearly other stuff Slimey had missed. The Bobby she thought she knew would never try to manipulate her into going backstage just so he could show off to his cabinmates, or steal her dress because she wouldn't kiss him.

As she inhaled to let out a sigh of frustration, the smell of manure filled her nostrils. She nearly gagged. *I'll deal with my stuff later*, she thought. She kissed the dangling silver locket, rose from her now unmade bed, and continued tracking the smell until she reached the bathroom.

"Ladies, it looks like we've been raided," Melman stated, inspecting the rest of the havocked beds and cubbies.

"Who did it?" Sophie asked.

"The San Juan boys! Jinx!" the J-squad answered in unison.

"But why?" Sophie asked.

"Uh, because they're immature boys who think they're funny," Melman responded.

Slimey wrapped a wad of toilet paper around her fingers and cautiously lifted the toilet lid. "Holy turds, you guys. They left . . . holy turds . . . in our bathroom!" She ran out as fast as she could.

"Omigod, gross!" Jenny, Jamie, Sophie, and Missi collectively moaned.

"All right, that's it!" Melman exclaimed, juggling her soccer ball on her thighs. "We've been waiting on the sidelines for this chance ever since we were One Tree Hillers. Anita Hill girls don't wait for anything. They strike while the iron's hot!" She excitedly headed the ball into the front door.

Missi jumped around spastically in agreement. "Raid them right this second! Let's go, team, go!"

Suddenly, a loud stomping came from the porch steps. The girls turned their heads toward the noise. Sara walked through the front door and gasped. "What the heck happened here?"

"The San Juan boys." Melman sighed. "They raided us."

Slimey looked to Melman, who was staring right back at her. She could tell they were thinking the same thing: Sara was never going to let them retaliate. Rick was the kind of counselor who allowed his campers to trespass and obliterate cabins, but Sara followed the rules. She might not have been awarded many Rubber Chickens in her time at Rolling Hills, but she sure hadn't found herself in the Captain's office, begging for a second chance.

But then she said, "Well, don't just stand there. What's the plan of attack?"

Melman and Slimey shared a mischievous smile.

Melman stepped forward. "We thought you'd never ask."

"All right, ladies, let's hustle." Melman clapped from the front door, desperately trying to get her bunkmates out of Anita Hill Cabin. The girls had skipped an entire Activity Period of lacrosse to plan the raid. Slimey had hoped they would come up with a unified strategy, but that didn't pan out. Sophie had a "secret strategy" she didn't want to talk about, Missi just wanted to go already, Jenny said she was too grossed out to think, Jamie was just happy to get out of lacrosse, and Melman was getting more frustrated by the second. By the time the bugle sounded, all they'd agreed to was to walk to San Juan Hill Cabin. As far as what would happen once they got there, well, that was still up for discussion.

"I'm not coming," Jenny announced, sprawled on her top bunk. The boys hadn't even stolen much of her stuff, but apparently their breaking and entering was traumatic enough.

"Can you at least be lookout, J?" Melman asked.

"I thought we decided I was lookout because of my night-vision binoculars," Sophie said.

"It's daytime," Slimey responded flatly. She had little to no patience right now.

"Are we all set?" Sara interrupted, charging through her beaded curtain. It was the most gung ho Slimey had seen her all summer. "Jamie, up front with Melman. Jenny, take caboose. Missi, in the middle. Whatever you wanna be in charge of is fine. Let's go!"

Jenny scrunched her nose in fake pain as she peeled herself from her bed and joined her cabinmates by the door. Sara held it open, and the girls marched out, striking various warrior yoga poses and determined to kick some serious San Juan butt. Melman jogged backward like a soccer coach, Slimey made sure her best friend didn't bump into a tree, Sophie had a first-aid kit strapped to her chest, Missi offered to meow if there were signs of danger, Jenny had padded her bikini with toilet paper as a sexy decoy, and Jamie was in charge of nothing.

As they ascended Harold, the second hill of the journey, Melman gave Sara a high ten. "I can't believe you're letting us do this."

"Exactly. You can't believe it, and neither will Rick."

"So this attack's about him?"

"You heard him at the beginning of the summer. 'Oh, Sara, you and your sour 'tude. Such a Debbie Downer. Is it because you can't get over Todd?' Well, it's time I proved him wrong."

"Yeah, but no one touched *your* stuff, Sara," Missi said.

"But they touched yours! And you girls have been my campers for two summers. No one touches Anita Hill's stuff, or they have to deal with me!"

"Yeah!" Melman and Missi cheered.

"What does Rick expect you to do?" Missi asked. "Just keep quiet about his campers vandalizing our cabin?"

"He probably didn't think about it. Boys don't think. And then they hurt you. I'm over guys and their stupid games. And now Rick's gonna be all 'Don't do it, Sara! Come on! Captain Hook'll give me kitchen duty for a whole week! It wasn't that much of a mess!' and I'll be like, 'Oh, yeah? Then why don't your boys come over and clean it up?' and he'll be like, 'Have you seen them clean?' and I'll be like, 'No, because—news flash—we're not allowed in each other's cabins!'"

Melman and Missi clapped at Sara's performance.

She giggled to herself. "It's a cutthroat world out there, girls, and everyone suffers when karma's chilling on the other side."

"It's a cutthroat world" rang in Slimey's ears as she drifted into a whirling Jacuzzi of painful thoughts about Bobby and what he'd done. She replayed the moment in her mind when she'd opened up to him about her locket and her dad. In spite of that heart-to-heart, he'd schemed behind her back, taken her stuff, and made her feel like she could never trust anyone again. What was he thinking? *He wasn't*, she told herself, echoing Sara's theory.

Slimey could feel her face getting hot and her eyes going glossy. Sure, she could tell Melman some stuff, but the really sad stuff . . . that was staying inside. *It was never OK to show it, not even to Bobby. Look at what good that did.* Now she was just more hurt.

She wiped her palms on her shorts and tucked some loose hair behind her ear. She supposed Sara was right. Karma was chilling on her side now. And if Bobby wanted to be all cutthroat by stealing her stuff, then so would she.

"Who wants to do the honors?" Sara asked.

They'd arrived at San Juan Hill before Slimey had even noticed. "I will!" she said fiercely before anyone else could answer.

"All yours, Slimey. Make strong choices. I'll be lookout."

Slimey marched up the six steps leading to the porch. Even though the cabin looked familiar from the outside, the porch was crammed with everything from hockey sticks to empty chocolate-milk cartons to T-shirts caked in mud hanging over the railing. She stopped at the front door and put her ear against the wood. Nothing. She turned the knob and slowly pushed the door open. As she stepped inside, she couldn't tell which was more overwhelming: the smell or the sight. "I think somebody got here first," she called out.

"Omigod, it smells like boy in here," Jenny squealed from behind her.

"It's like they raided themselves," Missi observed in awe.

"I need to shower before I have an allergic reaction," Sophie said, pulling the neck of her T-shirt over her nose and mouth.

"Try not to breathe in their toxins, ladies," Melman advised. She took a knee. The girls followed. "Listen up. Our opponents have dropped the ball in our court and poop in our toilet. Let's get them back. Divide and conquer on *three*. One, two, three . . ."

"ANITA HILL!!!" The girls sprang to their feet, then fanned out into the cabin.

Slimey scanned the room for Bobby's bed. The top bunk in the far left corner had a bunch of batteries, a crushed metal disk with a Swiffer pad stuck to it, and a remote control strewn across an unmade bed. *Steinberg.*

Below was an equally messy bed with Ritz cracker crumbs in the folds of a green comforter. Slimey looked closer to find melted gummy worms plastered to the pillow. A series of sticky fly traps filled with dead flies hung over half the bottom bunk. She full-on gagged and prayed this bed belonged to Play Dough and not Bobby, who she used to like, almost sort of kissed, even.

She took a few leaps toward the center of the cabin. The middle bunk-bed had an army-like sleeping bag neatly rolled up and fastened at the foot of the top bunk. A sash with Boy Scout pins and patches draped down over the ladder. *Dover's* . . .

Below was a bed with a basketball and tennis racket on top of a sports-themed comforter. Most boys were into sports, but in San Juan Hill Cabin it could've only been Totle's, or maybe Bobby's. But Bobby didn't love all sports, just baseball.

She took three giant steps toward the bunk-bed closest to the bathroom. The bottom bunk was freakishly neat compared to the disastrous state of the rest of the cabin. It was black and red, and the clothes in the cubbies nearby were color-coordinated. *Is Bobby that clean?* Slimey wondered. She doubted it and figured it was Wiener's. Up top was a blue comforter with orange pillows and a poster of a Mets baseball player swinging a bat. *Yes! That's it!*

Melman interrupted Slimey's investigation with the blow of a whistle. Slimey swiveled on her heels to see her bunkmates hopping around the cabin, avoiding the guys' mess like the plague. "Time out, ladies! Time out," Melman called. The girls turned her way. "Observation period is up. What's the set play?" The girls answered with blank stares. "Remember, this is our counterattack. Nothing too precious is out of bounds. There are no penalties. There are no fouls."

"Um, it actually smells *really* foul in here," Jamie said, as if that hadn't already been established.

"Look, it's time to get real! How can we win this?"

"Omigod, we should totally steal something," Jenny said.

"Yes! A *steal*!" Melman cried.

"Well, I know what I'm taking," Slimey said, her hand already in Bobby's stuff.

Melman blew her whistle. "All right, play on!"

Slimey rummaged through Bobby's cubbies and shelves and found postcards, envelopes, a baseball uniform, camp gear, sweatshirts, cologne, Surf Hair, and a torn picture of him when he was little—smiling wide on his dad's shoulders with his mom by their side. A piece of Scotch tape held it together. The last time Slimey saw Bobby smiling that wide was when they were dancing together. But he'd torn them apart, too, and something told her Scotch tape wasn't going to do the trick. She put the picture back where she'd found it and continued her search.

"Ew, ew, ew! Boy boxers!" Jenny clung to Dover's top bunk and pointed to a pile of underwear.

"That's it! Boxers!" Melman exclaimed. "Jenny for the golden goal! Round up all the underwear you can find . . ."

"Got it!" Slimey yelped, finally finding what she was looking for in Bobby's backpack—the one with his initials embroidered on it: *R.E.B.*

"You're taking his iPod?" Sophie asked.

"We are here to get revenge, right?" she asked the girls.

"RIGHT!" they shouted back.

Melman grabbed Wiener's pillow.

"What are you doing?" Missi asked.

"Watch and learn." Melman removed the pillow and stuffed the boys' underwear into the empty pillowcase.

"I can't believe you're touching their boxers with your bare hands," Jamie said.

"Do it like this," Missi advised, sticking her hand inside Totle's basketball-designed pillowcase, picking up a handful of underwear, and then turning the pillowcase inside out. "Like you're scooping up dog poop!" She swung it over her back.

"They're gonna beg, whine, and cry," Melman mumbled as she tried Missi's method. "It's gonna be glorious."

"Ew, what are you doing, Sophie?" Jamie asked.

Slimey turned toward Totle's bed to find Sophie sprawled across it on her stomach, her face in his sheets.

"I'm looking for paper."

"No, you're not. You're inhaling Totle's pillow."

"A human wouldn't understand." After a big whiff, Sophie picked up Totle's notebook from his top cubby. "All his dreams and thoughts about me must be inside of you," she whispered, bringing the cover to her lips. "I'll read you later in the dark."

Slimey had a feeling Sophie was going to be disappointed tonight.

Sophie ripped out a blank page, found a pen, and started writing.

"Nice one, Sophie!" Melman stood over her. "Tell the boys there's no limit to how far we'll go, and we're not backing down without a fight!"

"Wait, where's a good spot to leave the note?" Slimey asked, hopelessly scanning for an open area or at least a place the boys couldn't miss. Their cabin was so cluttered with junk, it could've been in an *I SPY* book.

"There isn't one," Jenny whined. "I doubt they'd find a note in here even if we told them where it was."

"I can write it with this." Sophie whipped out shiny red lipstick from the chest of her swimsuit.

"Did you just take lipstick out from your boobs?" Jenny asked with disgust.

"I thought that bump was your EpiPen," Slimey said.

"No, that's under my other boob."

"The mirror!" Melman yelled out. Inspired, she pulled Sophie up from Totle's bed. With lipstick in hand, they headed to the bathroom, kicking away whatever was in their way. Together, they stopped in front of the bathroom door and cried, "One,,two, three!" Inhaling deeply to hold their breath, they lunged inside.

The rest of the girls waited so silently, they could hear the flies buzzing around Play Dough's bed. A few seconds of itchy anticipation passed, and then Melman and Sophie emerged from the bathroom, gasping for air.

"It doesn't smell better out here! It doesn't smell better out here!" Sophie cried.

Melman pulled her in for a hug. "This girl here just wrote the sickest ransom note on the full-length mirror," she announced, smirking. "The San Juan Hill boys are gonna have to hunt their brains out to find their underwear!"

The girls jumped up and down in a loose huddle and let out a communal "WOOOO!" At Melman's short-short-long whistle blow, they sprang back into their warrior yoga poses.

"Where are we gonna hide their underwear?" Slimey asked Melman excitedly. She'd been thinking they were just going to store the boxers in the back of Anita Hill Cabin. Melman always made things more fun.

"Well . . . how do you ladies feel about—?"

Sara whistled her warning from the porch.

"Let's go! Let's go! Let's go!" the girls cried, frantically grabbing the pillowcases of dirty underwear. On the way out, they dumped whatever clothes were still in cubbies (and not already on the floor) to the floor.

As they sprinted and ducked behind Wawel Hill, Slimey turned to Melman with a grin. "So . . . where are we hiding their underwear?"

Melman leaned in and whispered the best hiding spot Slimey could NEVER think of. Slimey put her hand over her mouth and shook her head with glee. "You're good!" she whispered back, all smiles.

"Hell hath no fury like a woman scorned," Melman said. She crossed her arms over her chest and rolled down the hill in celebration. The girls followed suit, even Sara. "We did it, ladies. And this war has just begun!"

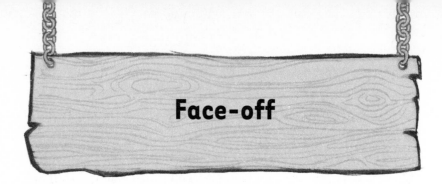

Face-off

"Hey, guys . . . I know I had more underwear than this," Play Dough said thoughtfully, standing by his bottom bunk.

"How much do you have?" Rick asked.

Play Dough picked up a heap of clothes from the floor and laid it on his bed. "One . . . One. I have one."

"Are you sure?" Steinberg asked. "That's a sock."

"I counted the ones I'm wearing."

Rick filled his cheeks with air and sighed it out loudly. "All right, boys, I'm pretty sure the girls have raided us back. Look through your stuff. See what's missing or messed up."

Please tell me no one touched my things, Bobby prayed. Filled with dread, he walked toward his cubbies.

Totle rummaged through his stuff. "Oh no! My underwear's gone, too!"

Bobby's clothes had been dumped from his cubbies to the floor, and, like the other guys, he couldn't find any underwear. He frantically searched through his remaining stuff.

"I think the girls took my high-thread-count Egyptian-cotton pillowcase," Wiener panicked. "Melman probably took it so she can smell me at night."

"Then Melman also loves me," Totle said. "My pillowcase is gone, too."

"Impossible."

"Possible. Plus my journal," Totle said.

Wiener rolled his eyes and headed toward the bathroom. For a split second Bobby was thankful he'd failed with Slimey so early on. Had they kissed, Totle would have written all about it in that same journal now in the girls' possession.

Bobby dumped whatever was inside his backpack onto the floor alongside his clothes. Out came six opened letters from his mom and dad, a picture of Clark Kent, two half-filled Gatorade bottles, an empty potato chip bag, a backup baseball mitt, a gray hoodie, a Rolling Hills T-shirt, and his headphones. His chest tightened. He knew exactly what was missing. "Where's my iPod? Did they steal my iPod, too?"

"Who would want your caveman iPod?" Play Dough asked.

Bobby didn't know. Who would want an old iPod? The battery ran out after forty-five minutes, and there was nothing on there that anyone but he or his dad listened to. Then again, maybe it was stolen for another reason. Maybe it was stolen because a certain someone who was mad at him knew how much it meant to him. How much it reminded him of his dad. How much he needed it when he was feeling sad. "Slimey, that's who."

"Heeeeeeeelp!" Wiener screamed bloody murder from the bathroom. Bobby dropped his empty backpack to the floor and raced inside. His cabinmates were right behind him. "It's written in blood!" Wiener stood in front of the full-length mirror, staring at a poem in big red letters.

Steinberg fastened his lab goggles over his face, smudged a letter with his thumb, and licked it. "Lipstick, not blood," he confirmed.

Play Dough pushed his way to the front and read it aloud.

Dear San Juan Hill Boys,

We had to raid you

It was only fair

Now we have your underwear.

If you want 'em back

You'll do what we say

Your boxers are hidden, like, real far away.

Your first clue

We have a hunch

Is where we eat our picnic lunch.

"Sounds like a treasure hunt," Steinberg said.

"Adventure-sauce!" Dover cried.

"It's not any 'sauce,'" Play Dough objected. "They stole our underwear. Any idea where we start, Steinberg?"

"Uh . . . yeah. It's in the riddle you just read."

"I can't believe Sara let this happen," Rick said. "She wants to fight dirty, let's fight dirty. Wiener, are the girls in their cabin?"

"Nope. Arts and Crafts."

"Perfect," Rick said ominously.

"Retaliation?" Play Dough asked.

"RETALIATION!" the other boys shouted, falling into a huddle. Bobby's arm made it in, but the rest of his body was stuck on the outside until Steinberg and Totle pulled him fully in.

As mad as Bobby was about his missing iPod, he was glad to be included with the guys. He was starting to see where Steinberg was coming from. Who cared about being cool? These guys might not have known everything about him, but they definitely knew something was up, and they hadn't teased or judged him for it. Meanwhile, judging them and judging himself had gotten Bobby nowhere. He supposed it was time to let go and be half as weird as everyone around him.

"They steal our stuff, we steal more of their stuff," said Play Dough.

"An eye for an eye," said Totle.

"A tooth for a tooth," said Dover and Steinberg.

"A spleen for a spleen," said Wiener.

"An iPod for a . . . something," Bobby stuttered. *I'll work on it*, he thought.

"Break out on *three*," Rick commanded. "One, two, three . . ."

"SAUCE!"

The guys formed a straight line and marched with determination out the front door of San Juan Hill Cabin, ready for Raid Number Two. And this time, Bobby didn't care what anyone said. He wasn't going to be lookout.

• • •

Ten minutes later, each of the guys was digging through a different cubby inside Anita Hill Cabin. Well, except for Totle, who was head-butting Melman's soccer ball against the back wall.

"Focus!" Play Dough warned. "We're running out of time!"

Totle put the ball down and dizzily stumbled into a bunk-bed post. "Time? It's definitely in the afternoon."

Play Dough shook his head. "Guys, just grab all their toiletries. If we're gonna stink wearing the same underwear over and over, then they deserve to stink, too!"

"See? I told you that taking their deodorant was a good idea," Wiener boasted.

Bobby fumbled through Slimey's stuff: hair ties, a brush, a handheld mirror, a squishy stress ball, flowery stationery, a half-made hemp bracelet. He'd been pumped for revenge back at San Juan Hill, but actually doing it felt wrong.

"What have you got, Smelly?" Play Dough asked.

"I mean, there's her roller-hockey knee pads . . . or I could take her stamps?"

"Dude, something she'll actually miss."

"What's that?" Dover asked.

Bobby did a one-eighty. "What?"

Dover pointed. "Dangling in front of your face?"

The swinging locket above Slimey's bed. Bobby didn't care if she'd stolen a hundred iPods, he would never take something that important to her. He would have to be the biggest, meanest bully in the world. "It looks like a plain old locket."

"It looks like revenge for your plain old iPod," Play Dough said, raising his eyebrows mischievously.

"Nah. I'll take something else."

"Fine, then, I'll take it."

Great, Bobby thought. If Play Dough took the locket, it would surely get lost in his mess of fly traps and candy wrappers. But if he took it, he'd look like the bad guy.

"They're coming back, boys!" Rick shouted from the porch.

What should I do, what should I do, what should I do? Bobby panicked.

"Let's move!" Rick yelled.

Bobby made his decision. "Forget it. I'll take it. My battle to fight—my locket to steal." Play Dough gave him an encouraging nod. Since Bobby's mesh shorts had no pockets, he slipped the locket around his neck. It felt cool against his skin. He untucked it and held it out from his chest.

"You OK, dude?" Play Dough asked, cracking his neck.

"Oh. Yeah. I'm fine." Bobby shuffled past him. *You have no choice. You're doing the right thing*, he told himself. *Keep the locket safe for Slimey.*

Steinberg removed the used garbage bag from the front of the cabin, dumped its contents onto the floor, and refilled it as fast as he could with the girls' soap, shampoo, and conditioner. Totle rushed out from the bathroom with a skinny cotton thing up his left nostril and knocked into Bobby.

"What happened to you?" Play Dough asked him.

"My nose started bleeding."

"Why is there a stringy thing on the gauze?" Dover asked.

"Because it's a tampon," Wiener said, grinning madly.

"Ewwwww!" the guys moaned as Totle ripped it from his

nose. Bobby was too nervous about the locket to get involved.

"Boys!" Rick threw open the front door. "It's go time. For real, they're coming!"

Steinberg and Totle carried the toiletries, Play Dough wrapped himself in a boy-band poster from the wall, Wiener tooted Missi's flute, and Dover carried a box of tampons. He caught Bobby looking.

"Free gauze, dude."

"Yeah, I know," Bobby said.

As the guys climbed up Anita Hill, they saw the girls at the top, explosively chanting like lunatics. "Anita Hill! Anita Hill! Anita Hill!"

The guys chanted back even louder. "San Juan Hill! San Juan Hill! San Juan Hill!"

Bobby couldn't help but look at Slimey, sandwiched between Melman and Jenny. Her eyes were focused on Play Dough and Totle, Dover and Steinberg, Wiener, even. But not him. She was deliberately avoiding him. Still.

"Anita, Anita, Anita!"

"SJH, SJH, SJH!"

Bobby kicked at the grass. *You know what, Slimey?* he thought. *You stole my dad's iPod, and all I did was keep watch, hoping like an idiot no one touched your stuff.* He wiped the sweat from his eyes in case anyone mistook it for tears.

"We've got all your toiletries!" Steinberg boasted.

"Now you'll know what it feels like to be dirty!" Totle shouted.

"Yeah, well, we've got all your underwear!" Melman taunted back, inching closer.

The boys marched past the screaming girls. Bobby swung the locket around his neck, so it dangled down his back, and averted his eyes. He was over this dumb raid war.

As he passed Melman, he heard her say, "Slimey, check out what Smelly has hanging down his back." Without even looking, he could feel a furious Slimey storming toward him. Her hair smelled like roses and chlorine.

"You took my dad's locket?! How could you?"

Play Dough fought back. "You took his iPod! What did you expect?"

"Again, this is between me and Bobby and no one else," Slimey snapped. She finally looked at him, right in the eye. "Now give it back!"

Because she was angry, Bobby was angry, and now he didn't want to give back her locket at all. He knew how it looked, but was she forgetting who he was? Forgetting all the time they'd spent together? Did she really think he'd take it without a good reason? "No!" Bobby shouted back, the sweat really pouring from his eyes.

"Are you crying?" Play Dough asked. "Rick!"

Rick rushed over. "What's going on?"

"Make him give back my dad's locket!" Slimey yelled.

"Make her give back my dad's iPod!" Bobby shouted over her.

"Whoa, whoa, chill." Rick put a hand on each of their backs and walked them a few feet from their cabinmates. "Keep walking, guys," Rick said to the rest of the San Juan Hillers. "We'll catch up in a minute."

"All right, girls, you, too," Sara called out over her shoulder as she headed toward Bobby and Slimey. "Inside Anita Hill while I talk to these two."

"Have fun finding your underwear, princesses!" Melman teased.

"Oh, we will. And once we do, you're gonna wish you had never started this war!" Dover shouted back.

"You started it, cheese-brain," Sophie laughed.

"Ignore her, Major Dover," Play Dough said.

Rick gave the guys time to disappear over the hill before he confronted Bobby. "Well . . . ?"

"What? I'm not giving anything back until I have my iPod."

"You of all people . . . ," Slimey said sharply, folding her arms over her chest.

"I had to take something!"

"You know how much that locket means to me."

"Yeah, but the guys—"

"Take responsibility for your actions, Bobby."

"Why don't you take responsibility? You stole my iPod!"

"Because I was mad at you!"

"You stormed out on me! You made me look like an idiot!"

"You ACTED like an idiot."

Bobby supposed she was right—he should've never pressured her to go backstage—and here he was, acting like a jerk all over again. He was tired of being the bad guy. "You know what? Here—just take your locket. I was gonna give it back, anyway. I only took it in the first place to keep it safe from the guys." He flung Slimey's necklace at her, and she caught it against her stomach. "Now you never have to talk to me again!"

Bobby fell to the ground, buried his head in his hands with shame, and rubbed his eyes. He couldn't pretend it was sweat anymore. It was obviously dumb tears he wished would just stay put. Rick squatted down by his side.

"Sara and I are gonna let you two have some alone time to figure this out."

Bobby gave him a look that obviously meant *No, please don't leave me alone with her,* but Rick got up anyway.

Bobby put his head down and picked at the grass. Slimey knelt down slowly. He wasn't looking at her, but he could tell out of the corner of his eye that she was looking away. They sat in silence for what felt like eternity plus a bunch of boring Social Studies classes.

"Hey. Here," Slimey said with a cracking voice, her hand outstretched, offering Bobby his dad's iPod.

"You had it on you?" he asked with surprise, taking it from her slowly.

"I snuck it to Arts and Crafts. To hear some of the songs."

"Why?"

"Because even though I'm mad at you, I still . . . like you."

Wait—you do? Bobby wondered if he'd heard her right.

"And I want to know more about you. You can tell a lot about a person by what songs he listens to."

Slimey already knew more about him than anyone else at Rolling Hills. He wondered what else she could possibly discover about him through his music. "So, what did you learn?"

"That you have an old-school iPod with really old-school songs . . ."

Bobby smiled. "I know. It's a twenty-gig, second generation. It's my dad's old one with all his favorite songs."

"That makes sense. I mean, I get why listening makes you think of him."

"Yeah, except, like, there's this song on here—'Michelle,' by the Beatles. Every time I hear it, it reminds me of when we played the marshmallow game together, 'cause, I dunno, it was the last song I listened to before I fell asleep that night. It doesn't make a lot of sense."

"No, it does."

"'Cause I just think of— I mean, it makes me think of you. And then there's this other one—it's called 'Layla.' I was listening to it when you came over to talk to me on the bleachers."

"You think about all those times?"

Of course I do. I like you, Slimey. I wanted to be your boyfriend, remember? He lowered his eyes to the iPod. "It's cheesy, but most of the songs on my iPod make me think of you."

Slimey's cheeks turned a shade of pink, and even though Bobby couldn't see his own face, he could feel it turning reddish, too.

"Bobby, did you really take my locket to protect it?"

"Yeah. Play Dough was gonna take it. I didn't know what else to do."

"What about my Midsummer Dance dress?"

"It was pretty . . ."

"That's why you took it?"

"I didn't take it. I was lookout the first time."

"Oh." Slimey looked down and picked at the grass just like

Bobby had been doing a minute ago. He could tell she felt bad for thinking the worst of him.

"Is that why you took my iPod? Because you thought I took your dress?"

Slimey looked up at him with her dark, apologetic eyes. She tried to say something, but she couldn't make the words come out.

Now Bobby felt guilty that she felt guilty, since he'd started the whole fight when he asked her to go backstage. "You know that night at the dance?"

"I know. I'm sorry."

"For what? I'm the one who messed up big-time. I shouldn't have let Play Dough or anyone else get in the way."

"That's true. I just kinda wish I hadn't gotten so mad. It's just that what our friends were all trying to do was . . . forced, you know?"

"Yeah. Jamie can't like me like . . . like how maybe you like me, because Jamie and I have never talked alone."

"I know! Right? But me and you. We click. I've told you things I haven't even told Melman."

"You have?"

"Don't tell her that." Slimey stuck out her pinky finger. Bobby gave her a clueless look. "Hook your pinky to mine and shake."

As their pinkies collided, Bobby could feel the electricity he'd felt when they were slow-dancing at the Midsummer Dance. But instead of it feeling amazing, like last time, now it just felt wrong. If Slimey was going to let herself trust him after what he'd done, he knew he'd better tell her the whole truth about himself. She might think he was a freak and never talk to him again, but better that happen now than later. He unlocked his pinky and scooted back.

"What's wrong?"

"Slimey, I really want to be honest with you, so we can start fresh."

"All right . . ."

"You know how I once told you it's OK to show you're sad?"

"Yeah."

"And I said how I'm bad at hiding how I'm feeling?"

"Yeah?"

"Well, I'm bad at it for a reason."

"Because of your stuff with your parents?"

"Well, yeah, that's part of it, but also I have . . ." He could feel his chest collapsing inward, his heart pounding a million miles per hour, his face getting hotter and redder.

"What do you take for it?"

"What?"

"Or do you just see a therapist?"

"Oh. I—well, I—" Slimey had caught him completely off guard. *How did she know?* "I used to go to a therapist, but then it wasn't working that good, so I started taking these blue tablet things that help me not freak out."

"Do you take them at camp?"

"I almost did. My mom sent them up a few days ago, but I didn't want anyone to ask why I was going to the infirmary after breakfast, so I haven't taken them yet."

"Why don't you just tell the truth? Are you that afraid of what people might think?"

"Yeah, I have anxiety over it."

Slimey laughed, which eased Bobby's chest of some of the tightness.

"I'm confused. Did someone tell you?"

"No. It's just that you said you can't hide your feelings, and it makes you feel weird, and you're bad at it for a reason, so I put the pieces together. It's not like you're the first person to have anxiety. My mom gets it. Ever since my dad passed, she's been on all sorts of pills."

"But if getting upset isn't weird to you, why do you hide your sadness at camp?"

"I dunno. It makes people feel awkward or bad for me. They try to understand, but they can't. And sometimes there's someone who comes along who *does* understand, and it feels amazing. But if that person lets you down, you hurt even more."

"Like how I hurt you?"

Slimey bit the inside of her cheek and averted her eyes, which told him the answer was yes. A wave of guilt and regret crushed Bobby. The way he'd acted at the Midsummer Dance was a jerk move, but to Slimey, it had been upsetting on a whole other level. She'd trusted him with personal stuff she didn't even tell Melman, and once she opened up—once he encouraged her to open up—he'd hurt her all over again.

"But it's OK," she continued. "Camp is the place I go to get away from all that."

All Bobby wanted to do in that moment was hold her, tell her everything was going to be OK, promise to never hurt her again, and swear he'd be there for her whether she was happy or sad.

"Slimey?" She looked deep into his eyes, and even though they weren't touching, the electricity was working just the same. "I'm so sorry. If you'll forgive me, I promise to be there for you. So you don't have to be the strong one all the time. I can be the strong one, too. Sure, I might have a panic attack in the middle of it, but—"

"You already are." Slimey inched toward Bobby like she was going to whisper something in his ear.

He leaned forward, but instead of a whisper he felt a gentle touch on his cheek. *Did Slimey just kiss me? Did SLIMEY just kiss ME? DID SLIMEY JUST KISS ME?!*

She drew back with a smile, stood up, and walked away toward Anita Hill Cabin. "See you later, Bobby," she said over her shoulder.

Bobby followed her with his eyes, just as he'd followed her after she'd stormed out of the Social Hall during the dance. But this time, the hotness in his face felt awesome. He tried to say something really cool or nice or sweet or smart or anything, really, but he was too stunned to speak. Instead, all that came out was a high-pitched squeak.

Her ponytail swooshed as she turned around.

Say something, Bobby! "Yeah, you . . . you too," he stuttered.

Slimey nodded with a big smile and skipped down the hill, glowing even from behind.

July 26th

Dear Mom + Dad,

Revealing too much information

might be dangerous for you, but

just know, the Boy Scouts have

gotten me ready for war.

Ben

August 1st

Dear Mom,

How are you? Camp's amazing!!! So much has happened since my last letter, I don't know if I'll be able to fit it all in.

I am almost done with four Arts & Crafts projects, and I can't wait to finish them. One is a jewelry box, one is a picture frame, one is a painting of the hills with, like, a really pretty orange sunset, and one is for you, so it's a surprise . . . Oh, that reminds me, I got your package. It's great! But you don't have to sew candy into teddy bears anymore like last summer. TJ's been checking instead of the Captain, and he doesn't care about that stuff. As long as we share and don't have an infestation of skunks.

One last thing, because I'm running out of room: Remember that cute friend I told you about? I know I said we're not friends anymore, but that was last week. Now he's my boyfriend. I know you might say I'm too young or something, but don't worry, you'll like him :). He's really nice.

Love to you and Lois Lane. I just remembered a trick if she's still not eating her seeds. Put them in that small blue measuring cup. Sometimes that works. Miss you!

Love,
Stephanie

5 August

Dear Little Ealing Fireflies,

Whassup? Tired yet from all the ladder sprints in Regent's Park? Because of my kick-butt sweeper skills, Camp Rolling Hills made the fourteen-and-up girls' championship! Just kidding—we lost after the first game. We don't have players like you here. But still, I played my best, and it was so fun. Only thing is, and don't be mad, I lost my uniform. It was in my cubby, nice and safe, and then the stupid boys our age stole it to be funny. Probably this one kid, Wiener, who's obsessed with me. I'll get it back, but it's kind of messing with my head right now, since it's so important to me. I miss you girls! Tell Coach Sully I say, "Soccer sock it to me, baby."

    Kick butt, always.
    #24,
    Melman

August 6th

Dear Journal 2,

It's a good thing I brought you to camp as a backup, since the girls stole your twin brother. I hope they're learning all of my philosophies on life. If they embrace my wisdom, your brother will be back in no time.

Remember S.T.A.R.F.I.S.H.? This is how I'm applying it.

S is for Sportsmanship.

    No spitting in the girls' hands after games.

T is for Tolerance.

    Tolerate the girls.

A is for Appreciation.

    Appreciate our underwear.

R is for Respect.

    Respect the hunt.

F is for Friendship.

    Hunt with friends.

I is for Integrity.

    I always forget what this one means.

S is for Sensitivity.

    Don't cry in front of the girls.

H is for Helpfulness.

    Help the girls learn they're wrong.

                         Don't disappear, too,

                         Totle

Dear Georgina Whitefoot,

Unfortunately, I think your letter back to me got lost. The mail system here needs a lot of improvement. Anyway, since my last letter, I've finished reading <u>Howling at the Sun, Part III</u>, and duh, I LOVED it! I have a lot more questions, though.

- Was Axel possessed by demons when he bought the wooden bullets?
- Are you writing a fourth book?
- When did you write your first book?
- Was it about vampires?
- Why was it about vampires?
- Do I have a chance at finding love even if everyone's a human?
- I like to pretend I'm a vampire, but I'm not, cause I can digest mac 'n' cheese, right?

Here's the gossip update:

I still like Totle. I stole his journal. He didn't write about me, but I can tell that he's thinking about me in every sentence he writes. I haven't bitten his neck yet, mostly cause I haven't danced with him since the Midsummer Dance, but that option's still on the table if you think it's right.

Your BIGGEST, BIGGEST, BIGGEST fan,
Sophie Edgersteckin

Something Fishy

TJ: Good morning, Camp Rolling Hills! Just a few brief announcements before we launch into this beautiful day.

Captain: TJ, they need you right now!

TJ: Yours truly will be joining Nurse Nannette in the infirmary to tend to the brave little boys of Bunker Hill Cabin who were singed by last night's fireworks.

Captain: On behalf of our entire staff, we apologize. They were supposed to explode in the sky.

TJ: But worry not: Nurse Nanette tells me the Bunker Boys will be back to playing games and NOT LISTENING TO THEIR COUNSELORS soon enough.

Captain: You . . . don't have to include this incident in your letter home if you don't want to.

TJ: Instead, you can ask your parents for a donation of underwear for the stinky boys of San Juan Hill Cabin. They smell really bad.

Captain: Please do not ask for donations of underwear. That's . . . strange.

TJ: You're right. Take the day off from letter-writing!

Captain: That's not what I—[*feedback squeal*]

Slimey was tucked beneath her covers, shirt over her nose, inhaling the shallowest of breaths. The Anita Hillers were halfway through Rest Hour and stuck with the wretched smell of dead fish that had been seeping into the cabin walls, their clothes, and, grossly enough, their hair over the past six days. They had tried to seek haven in the infirmary, but it was currently taken up by the stomach flu-ed Tyler Hillers and the lice-infested One Tree Hillers. When that plan failed, Melman suggested sleeping outside, but it had been pouring all week.

Slimey imagined the war would have fizzled out naturally if only TJ hadn't endorsed a search for the San Juan Hill guys' underwear, spreading the challenge to the entire Boys' Side for a prize of free Canteen for a week (that's how bad the San Juan Hillers stunk). The mass scavenger hunt had escalated the battle to crazy heights, and the Captain had been trying to rein in Boys' Side over the last two days, cracking the whip on any and all raid business.

But Play Dough had still managed one last prank. And when Jenny had harassed him about it in the Dining Hall, all he'd said was "As long as we're boxer-less, the war's still on!"

It was official. The San Juan Hill boys and the Anita Hill girls were at a standstill. The girls had the boys' underwear, but they also had a rotting fish hidden somewhere in their cabin. There was nothing left to do but compromise. Miserable, the girls listened to Sara bawl out Rick on the front porch.

"Really, Rick? A dead fish?"

"You're the one who initiated a treasure hunt, Sara."

"Since when is dirty underwear treasure?"

"Oh, it's treasure when you have six twelve-year-olds walking around with no underpants on!"

"We've looked everywhere. You gotta get it out!"

"I thought we weren't allowed in the girls' cabins."

"Just get the stinking fish, Rick!"

"Not until you give back the underwear. Is this about Todd?"

Sara let out a scream of frustration, but Slimey knew that Rick was right. This wasn't just about the fish. Slimey thought back to the heart-to-heart she'd had with Sara on the Anita Hill porch steps right after Bobby had given back her locket.

"You forgave him, just like that?" Sara had asked, biting her nails. "You were able to just let it all go?"

Slimey had smiled. "Yeah. Holding a grudge hurts more, I think."

Sara had considered this. "But what if the grudge is justified? Like, what if he embarrassed you and dumped you and then bragged to his friends about it?"

"Todd bragged to his friends about dumping you?"

"I dunno. Probably. Guys are the worst."

Slimey had bitten her lip, wanting to tell Sara she was being silly, but she didn't want to make her feel bad. "Not all guys are like Todd. And even if he did brag to his friends, it doesn't mean they thought it was cool. They probably think he's dumb for dumping you."

"Like Rick? You think he thinks Todd is dumb?"

Slimey wasn't sure about that—Rick and Todd were best friends, after all. But she could tell Sara needed this. She'd nodded a yes.

"Yeah. You're totally right. That's why Rick's been so nice to me—because he feels bad I dated his dumb friend! 'Poor, pathetic, dumped Sara,' he's probably thinking."

"I don't think that's why Rick's nice to you," Slimey had said. "He probably just thinks you're really cool."

Sara had looked at her inquisitively. "Who are you, Slimey? How am I getting the best advice ever from a twelve-year-old?"

As the fight outside reached record levels, Slimey came back to reality. She pulled her covers up to her eyes as Rick and Sara scream-ranted at each other. It appeared Sara hadn't taken the heart-to-heart as much to heart as Slimey had hoped.

The fight sounded like:

"Oh, yeah? Well, my boys haven't had a clean pair in over a week. They won't participate in any activity other than your nonsensical hunt. They're obsessing over all of it, and it's driving me crazy. The clues are meaningless— it's like you wrote whatever arbitrary rhyme popped into your head. It's ridiculous! I am so close to hauling myself to Walmart and buying them all some fresh pairs."

"My girls will not sleep in Anita Hill tonight—I promise you that. Sophie's been so off the wall, she's been keeping her EpiPen in a ready-to-stab position, duct-taped to her thigh! And even though you thought you were being all noble when you left my stuff alone, unfortunately dead-fish smell infiltrates everything. So you're gonna need to get whoever did this back here to remove that stinking thing before I—"

Before you what, Sara? Slimey twiddled her thumbs for a few seconds, expecting Sara to speak up, scream out, stomp back inside, even. But all her ears registered was silence. She pulled her shirt down from her nose and cocked her head in the direction of the front door. "Does anyone know what's happening?"

"I dunno. Maybe they died," Jamie answered, pulling herself up from under Jenny's covers, where they'd been cuddle-spooning.

"Doubt it. But still, something is up . . . ," Melman said, hopping down from her top bunk and venturing toward the window. The J-squad and Missi followed.

"OMIGOD!!!" the J-squad screeched, their noses pressed against the glass. "Jinx! Double jinx! Triple jinx!" They broke into laughter and then coughed from the penetrating fish taste in the air. Normally, Melman would have given Slimey a *They deserved that* look, but ever since the raid, the J-squad had been a smidge more tolerable. A smidge.

"Sara and Rick are 'Sa-Rick'?!" Jenny grappled through her cough.

Slimey crawled out from her bottom bunk. As she peered out the window, she was totally stunned by what she saw. Sara was pushed up against the porch railing by Rick's body. His hands were holding her cheeks, her arms thrown around his neck, their lips meshing.

A grin crept across Slimey's face. When she was giving Sara advice to not close herself off to *all* guys, she'd never in a million years imagined it would come to this. *Well, to each his own—*

something her dad had always said when someone did something "out there."

"Omigod, I knew it the whole time," Jenny bragged, grabbing one of her hidden spare phones to take a picture.

"Oh, really?" Sophie said nasally, an earplug up each nostril. "Swear on Georgina Whitefoot's grave?"

"Who?" Jenny used all her strength to pull the window up. "We don't care that you two are making out. We really don't. But, please, can you get this freakin' fish out of our cabin?"

Sara and Rick awkwardly untangled their bodies. "Oh, hey, Jamie," Rick said, flustered.

"It's Jenny."

"Sara had a . . . a . . . I think her wisdom tooth is infected. I was just checking it out for her. My dad's a dentist, and—"

"Your dad's a park ranger. You told us last summer."

Sara smiled uncomfortably and slapped Rick on the back of the head. "I got you, girls. Don't worry." She looked him sharply in the eye. "Rick?"

"On it. I'll get Play Dough. He's the one who planted Mr. Fatty."

"Who's Mr. Fatty?" Sara asked.

"The fish."

"Gross."

Slimey didn't scrunch her nose in disgust like the rest of her cabinmates. Or join the squealing over Jenny's slide show of pictures she'd taken of Sa-Rick mid-kiss on her phone. Instead, she flopped onto her bed to be alone with her thoughts. Before she'd met Bobby, she'd convinced herself it was easier to just keep all her pain locked up inside. There was no point in opening up. It would just hurt more. But she realized now that there are people who can offer more than awkward pats and *I feel bad for you* smiles, and when they do, you're one step closer to having everything feel normal. She promised herself she'd never shut people out like Sara had almost done to Rick and she'd almost done to Bobby, because sometimes the ones you think are out to get you are really just trying to *get you.* Or . . . you know, kiss you.

Play Dough stood grandly in the doorway of Anita Hill Cabin. "Now, as to the matter of our underwear . . ." Dover stood over their stockpile of stolen goods: Jenny's dresses that Melman had "lent" them for Campstock, toiletries, clothes, and accessories.

"Go. Find it. Now," Rick commanded Play Dough.

"I will dispose of the fish in exchange for—"

"We'll exchange. Just get the fish!" Sara cut him off, holding a pillow over her face to mask the smell.

"No!" Dover protested. "I did not pull multiple all-nighters deciphering your clues, only to have you hand us the answer!"

Slimey wondered what deciphering Dover could have possibly been up to—the clues had been getting weirder and weirder, especially Missi's and Jamie's, and they kind of made no sense.

"Dude, the answer is our underwear," Play Dough pleaded.

"We can do this!" Dover shouted. "Don't give up, Play Dough! Never give up!"

"If you don't *want* your underwear, that's fine," Sara said. "But we're still keeping our stuff, and you're still removing the fish."

"Sorry, dude. I gotta," Play Dough said, taking a few dramatic steps toward the middle of the cabin, clearly enjoying the suspense. After a few turns, he stopped with his index finger pointing at Jenny's bed. Jenny's whole body stiffened with anger. Slimey was afraid she might grab Sophie's EpiPen to jab him with.

Play Dough brushed past Jenny to her bed, plopped down on his belly, and stretched his arm out as far as it would go. He pulled out the rotting Mr. Fatty. It was caked in dust bunnies. Jenny screamed as Play Dough obnoxiously paraded the slimy, smelly, lifeless fish through Anita Hill Cabin.

"Last chance, Dover," Rick said. "Smell yourself and then tell me you don't want to know where your underwear is hidden." Dover smelled himself and coughed. "And if that's not enough to change your mind, I also want to remind you that as of now we San Juan Hillers have no leverage over the—"

"Vive la guerre!" Dover shouted at the top of his lungs, his eyebrows twitching.

"No underwear it is. All right, buddy, let's get you some rest." Rick pushed Dover out by his shoulders, leaving the girls' stolen stuff behind.

Enough is enough. Slimey didn't care how stubborn Dover was—it was time the boy she liked smelled better than his nickname suggested. But before anything else, she had to talk to her soul sister. She slid her pink Chucks on, took Melman's hand, and led her to the bathroom.

"I went, like, ten minutes ago. I'm good," Melman said, rubbing her belly.

Slimey squeezed Melman's hand. "I'm sorry. You're my best friend, Melman. In the whole wide world. And in the beginning of the summer, I acted weird. I didn't tell you I liked Bobby, because you think boyfriends are dumb, and—"

"I don't think boyfriends are dumb."

Slimey lowered her eyes in disbelief. "But you said we don't need them."

"Yeah. We don't." Melman slid her hand from Slimey's and picked her calluses for what felt like an eternity. And then, another eternity later, she said, "But you can still tell me stuff, Slimes. I want you to."

Slimey nodded apologetically. She thought about how if Melman had a boyfriend she was sharing Twix bars with and spending all her time with and telling personal stuff to, it would totally feel like little stabbing pins and needles of betrayal. Slimey wished she'd thought about that earlier.

"But I'm glad you're coming to me now," Melman said, a few shades brighter. "Sorry. I should have been more supportive before. It's just . . . you know."

Slimey did know—now, at least. She hated that she'd hurt Melman, and she would do just about anything to make this awkward conversation stop and never come back and for the two girls to be hugging and laughing and joking like normal. "I'm really sorry, Mel."

"It's OK," Melman said, slipping her hand back into Slimey's. "And since the kid didn't steal your dress and didn't mean to be all like, 'Go backstage with me now, woman!' and he just really likes you and wants to kiss you, then—"

"What?!"

Melman gave Slimey the same mischievous eyebrows-up-and-down look that she'd given her and Bobby in the pool. Slimey shook her head and let out a chuckle of relief. Melman always seemed to know what Slimey was up to before she even said a word.

"But, Slimes? Next time, tell me. If you like someone, I mean. I don't like sharing you with someone I don't know squat about. For all I know, he could be addicted to piña coladas."

The girls broke into laughter. "Deal," Slimey said, flinging her arms around Melman and kissing her head over and over again.

"Save it for Bobby!" Melman squealed. The girls fell to the sticky bathroom floor, all tangled up and giggling. "Go!" Melman cried, giving Slimey a nudge.

"I'll tell you everything as soon as I'm back—I promise!"

"Maybe not everything . . . ," Melman said, scrunching her nose in playful disgust.

"Oh, it'll be everything." Slimey tapped her heart twice, and Melman did the same, before she hustled out the cabin door.

"Oh, let's face it, we're never gonna find 'em," **Play Dough** grumbled, peering aimlessly down the camp's dirt road.

"I don't get it," Steinberg said. "The girls offered to give us our underwear back, and you geniuses told them no?"

"The boxers have to be around here somewhere," Dover said maniacally, pulling himself out from under the Arts & Crafts porch. "We're so close, I can smell 'em."

"You're catching a whiff of *yourself*," Wiener said. "You haven't slept or showered in, like, a week."

"Dover's right!" Totle did his stroking-an-invisible-beard thing. "We shouldn't give up on our underwear. Our underwear would never give up on us!"

"That is just not true," Steinberg said with a groan, looking to Bobby for support.

Bobby nodded halfheartedly. Ever since he and Slimey had made up with a kiss on the cheek, and everyone had started calling them boyfriend and girlfriend, he was having a hard time caring about the hunt.

"Read the last clue, PD," Dover said.

Play Dough pulled a note from his shorts pocket and read:

Look up, look down, look all around,
Think where Picasso would chill.
Are you hungry for a cheeseburger?
Stay away from Forest Hill.

"It's obviously here!" Dover exclaimed.

"I'm hungry for a cheeseburger," Play Dough mumbled.

"But not as hungry as I am for our underwear," Totle said. "Absence makes the heart grow fonder."

"Aren't we next to Forest Hill?" Bobby pitched in.

"Exactly. Girls always say the opposite of what they mean," Totle informed him.

"Should we find cheeseburgers?" Play Dough asked.

"I'm going back under," Dover said, getting ready to dive below the Arts & Crafts shack again. "Who's with me?" Play Dough and Steinberg rolled their eyes as they knelt to the ground. Totle dropped into a push-up and rolled under.

"You guys go ahead," Wiener called after them. "Smelly and I are gonna take a look inside. Right, Smelly?"

"Sounds good to me." It did sound good to Bobby. Especially after Wiener had told him there was a family of hybrid skunk-chipmunks living underneath the porch. Skunk-munks he'd called them.

"FOUND IT!" Dover cried in a muffled voice.

"Our underwear?" Wiener asked. "You found our underwear?"

"No, dude! Another clue!"

"NOOOO!" Play Dough whined, crawling out from under the shack. "Enough with the clues! They go on forever and lead us nowhere!"

"Chill out, PD!" Dover said, emerging behind him. "Just listen:

This next adventure

Is not one to miss

Especially if you're waiting

For that special kiss.

"Backstage!!!" Play Dough shouted, grinning proudly and shaking Dover by his shoulders. "I've never been so smart in my life!"

"Dude, it's not over till our underwear is back in our possession," Steinberg said. "Let's check it out."

The boys set out on the dirt road leading to the Social Hall. Bobby hoped this was the last stop, but he knew Steinberg was right. They'd gotten their hopes up again and again, only to return to San Juan Hill Cabin empty-handed. Suddenly, Bobby heard someone trailing behind them.

"Hey, Bobby." He stopped short and smiled. He could've recognized her shampooed-hair smell and cheery voice anywhere.

He turned around, still smiling. "Hey, Slimey! What are you doing here?"

"We're about to find our underwear, woman!" Dover shouted. "And you can't stop us!"

"Oh, yeah? Where are you headed?"

"Wouldn't you like to know!" Dover screamed before darting ahead, dust flying at his heels.

"Good luck, Dover," Slimey called out to him with a grin. "Can I talk to you in private for a sec, Bobby?"

"Oh, yeah, sure."

"You coming, Smellsky?" Play Dough called back to him.

"Nah, go ahead. I'll meet you guys after." Bobby turned back to Slimey. "What's up?"

"Follow me." She grabbed his hand and led him in the opposite direction as the guys. They walked together for what seemed like fifteen minutes, even though he knew it was probably only five. It was just that his palms were really sweaty. He was telling himself not to sweat so he could continue holding Slimey's hand until she let go and not vice versa, but it was proving difficult. Especially as they walked up and down Sherri Hill and another hill Bobby couldn't remember the name of, through a forest clearing, past the Gazebo, and up to Baseball Field 2. "Now, close your eyes," she said softy, finally letting go.

Bobby did as he was told, and Slimey led him onto the field, her arm linked inside his like that very first Evening Activity, during the three-legged race. His heart was pounding. Bobby had no idea what to expect except that whatever was coming was probably good, based on her commitment to sweaty hand-holding these last several minutes.

"Do you know where we are?" she asked.

"At the baseball field . . . ?"

"But, like, more specifically?" A pause. "You can open your eyes if you want."

Bobby opened his eyes, and right in front of him was Slimey, with home plate in the distance. To his right was the pitcher's mound. He smirked. "We've reached first base, haven't we?"

"That's right," she teased.

Without thinking, without analyzing, without letting his nerves get to him first, Bobby leaned in to kiss her on the lips. She pulled back. *Please don't tell me I blew it again*, he prayed. *Please, please, please.*

Terrified, Bobby looked at her, hoping to find an answer. Hoping that answer was not another rejection. But there she was, looking back at him, smiling, her eyes sparkling. He could tell she was waiting for him to say something. Do something. *Should I try again?* he wondered. *Is Slimey flirting with me? Is this what flirting looks like?*

"First base stinks!" he said, attempting to flirt back but regretting it as soon as he said it.

She gave him a knowing nod. "It dooooes, doesn't it?"

Something about the slow, deliberate way she said it made him think she was talking about something other than the two of them. Bobby chewed his bottom lip. "Our underwear! Is it buried under first base?"

She recited the last clue: "*This next adventure is not one to miss. Especially if you're waiting for that special kiss.*"

"Does that mean yes?"

Slimey leaned in and kissed Bobby on the mouth. It lasted less than three seconds, but that was still enough time for him to taste her sweet-mint-gum-and-pizza breath and make his lips buzz with excitement. She pulled away slowly, their eyes opening and locking.

"There's a shovel by the bleachers, and I was never here," she whispered into his ear before running off, leaving him stunned after his first non-cheek kiss.

Bobby watched her go until she was out of sight, then skipped around first base like it was his fifth, sixth, seventh . . . heck, every great birthday he'd ever had, and he'd just consumed every inch of icing off the cake. He grabbed the shovel, raised it over his head, let out a manly howl, and got to work.

The Case of the Missing Underwear
Status: Solved

Bobby took a deep breath and brought the megaphone to his face. "Attention, Boys' Side. I have a very important announcement to make. The announcement you've all been waiting for. Gather round, gather round!" Bobby couldn't help grinning as his confused cabinmates emerged. They'd followed his voice to the Boys' Side Flagpole, where a crowd of male campers from Bunker Hill and Wawel Hill and every Hill cabin in between were already standing around with anticipation. He watched his cabinmates follow the other campers' gaze to the tip-top of the pole, where there was no flag, just Bobby, suspended in the air by his pants loop, spackled from forehead to ankles in dirt, megaphone in one hand, two pillowcases in the other.

"Is that what I think it is?!" Totle asked.

Bobby held up the pillowcases excitedly. Totle performed his victory dance.

"You found my high-thread-count Egyptian-cotton pillowcase!" Wiener shouted with relief.

"Well, that's not all," Bobby said through the megaphone. For the first time ever, his heart was racing with a different kind of anticipation, a kind he could get used to.

Totle took a second. "You got another fish?" he shouted up.

"No. I got this." In what felt like action-movie slow-mo, Bobby dumped the contents of the pillowcases onto the crowd of cheering, gagging boys and their counselors.

The San Juan Hill boys jumped up and down and onto one another with glee as they grabbed their hazardous boxers raining from the sky. TJ had stuck around after helping Bobby and was standing at the foot of the pole, arms crossed, hands in his armpits, grinning proudly.

"Oh, sweet, sweet undies, I thought I'd lost you forever," Steinberg mumbled to himself, collecting his favorite argyle pair.

"Where'd you find 'em?" Dover called up to Bobby, his eyelids and eyebrows twitching out of sync. "One Tree Hill Cabin?"

"Uh, yeah," Bobby said.

"I KNEW IT!" Dover paced around the pole. "We eat our picnic lunch by the picnic benches, which were originally outside Notting Hill Cabin, which is situated diagonally next to Tyler Hill Cabin, which sort of hangs over Two Tree Hill Cabin, which is the rebuilt cabin after the original One Tree Hill Cabin got burned down by an untended hair dryer in 1974!"

Steinberg cocked his head. "Dude, get some REM-cycle—"

"My logic, exactly," Bobby said into the megaphone.

Dover gave a twitchy smile.

"Good work, Sergeant Smelly," Play Dough shouted up. "Now what?"

With all the excitement, Bobby forgot how much pain he was in. "Can you get me down? This is starting to feel like a wedgie."

TJ lowered Bobby from the top of the flagpole, and once he was unhooked, all his cabinmates attacked him with fist bumps, high fives, and hugs. It didn't feel like the attack of enthusiasm he'd suffered on day one. It felt superhero amazing.

"I've gotta hand it to you," Play Dough said. "I never would've thought it, but you've found the weirdest way to make camp history."

"Yeah, well, I couldn't have done it without you guys. In the beginning of the summer, you couldn't pay me off in World Series tickets to do something like this."

"So, how do you feel?" Totle asked, wearing his pillowcase as a bandana.

Bobby took a deep breath. "Crazy! Plus, my butt crack hurts."

The guys doubled over with laughter.

"Residual pain from a wedgie lasts no more than forty-eight hours," Steinberg assured him, stretching his hand out for a shake. "You're a cool guy, Smelly."

Bobby felt his chest expand. "Right back atcha, Steinberg." They shook. "Oh, man, I can't wait to tell Keith and Jake about this."

"Who?" Play Dough asked.

"My best friends from home. They'll think this is hilarious."

"No, they won't," Steinberg said. "If you explain this to any-one at home, you'll sound super-lame."

"Super-lame? How?"

"Let's start with your nickname."

Bobby let out a laugh. "True."

"And what did you do, exactly, that you're so proud of?" Steinberg asked.

"I dug up a pillowcase of dirty underwear that the girls stole from us!" Bobby said proudly.

"See my point?"

"Oh. Yeah, it's weird."

Steinberg put his arm around Bobby. "Yup. We're all a bunch of really cool weirdos."

Bobby looked at him, nodded appreciatively, and put his arm around Steinberg.

"Group hug?" Totle proposed, picking Steinberg up via a wedgie.

"Hey! Ow!" he laughed.

Bobby held Steinberg's legs, relieving him of wedgie-pain, Dover wrapped his arms around all of them, Wiener jumped onto Dover's back, and Play Dough came in with a bear hug, knocking them all to the ground. Bobby closed his eyes and tried to relish all the good stuff from this summer, like Rick teaching him guitar, and Dover's raid map, and Steinberg's probably-genius inventions, and Totle's diary, and Wiener's classy dandelion he'd taped to his shirt for the Midsummer Dance, and Play Dough's ginormous poop baby he'd made just for the girls. But Bobby didn't want to go back in time. More than anything, he just wished this moment could last forever.

Aug 17th

Dear Christopher,

How r u? I know it's like really weird I'm writing you this (LOL), but I just want to confirm our relationship name. Here are some options for you to choose from:

Christo-Jenny
Jenny-Christo
Jennipher (OMG, that's like actually my real name, except I spell it Jennifer!)
Pher-Jen (say that really fast—what does it sound like?!? Ha-ha-ha-ha-ha-ha!)

XOXO,
Jenny

Aug 17

Dear Mom & Dad,

Camp's good.

From,

Robert Steinberg

CAMP ROCKS!

Date: _Aug 18_

Dear _Grandpa Jerry and_ ,
      Step-Grandma Sally,

How are you? I am ☹ _camp's over_.
                        soon
Camp is _over soon. I just wrote that_.

Today we _shaved our legs with_ .
                  whipped cream
My favorite thing so far is _____

_____ _Jen-Jam. DUH._ _____.

My cabin is _Oh, Anita Hill_ .

The food is _made in the kitc_hen

Write back soon! Actually don't. Camp
                 will be over, and I'll
From,   never get your letter.
   Jamie

August 19th

Dear Dad,

I can't believe tomorrow morning I'll be leaving camp. Summer here goes by really fast. My girlfriend, Slimey, is really cool, and I can't wait for you to meet her. I don't know how far Hoboken is from her house, but she lives in NJ, so it can't be that far. Also, I finally mastered the song I wrote on the guitar. It sounds really good. I think you'll be proud.

I also want to tell you that it's OK you moved out. Just try not to be so hard on Mom.

I miss you, Dad. Play catch and help me practice pitching when I'm home?

Love,
Bobby

August 19th

Dear Mom,

It's crazy that tomorrow we're out of camp. Now I can't imagine being anywhere else. My girlfriend, Slimey, is really sweet, and I think you'll like her. Everyone does. Also, I finally mastered the song I wrote on the guitar. It sounds awesome.

I also want to tell you that even though I never took the meds you sent up, I made it through the summer, and it was great.

Can we have cheesesteak for dinner tomorrow with whole-fat mozzarella? I miss real food.

Love,
Bobby

All the Songs on My iPod Make Me Think of You

Bobby glanced at the San Juan and Anita Hill campers around the campfire, their lit faces distorted by the rising smoke. The flames pressed heat against his cheeks, warming him from the late-night chill. He watched Rick and Sara distribute sticks and s'mores supplies, and he moved closer to Slimey on the log. Her hair smelled like it always did, mixed with the sweet scent of burning wood.

> **TJ:** Another fantastic summer at Camp Rolling Hills is all too quickly coming to an end.
> **Captain:** Before I forget, congrats to Robert Steinberg. Your mother called. She got your postcard. She's glad "Camp's good."

Melman gave Steinberg a high five.

> **TJ:** We're also happy to hear that the boys of San Juan Hill are back in clean undies. I was starting to feel bad about gagging in their presence.

The guys and girls cheered wildly.

> **Captain:** Which reminds me, don't forget to check the lost-and-found.
>
> **TJ:** I'm keeping everything you kids don't claim!
>
> **Captain:** And remember—tomorrow night at ten o'clock, step outside your home, look at the moon, and sing our alma mater. It's my favorite Rolling Hills tradition.
>
> **TJ:** You're my moon, Captain.

There was the brief yet disturbing sound of grown-ups making out, and then the PA went off with its signature piercing squeal.

"Get a room!" Play Dough shouted, making everyone laugh.

Slimey pulled her twig out of the fire, brought two flaming marshmallows to her mouth, and blew. They were brown and white, and they gooed right off the twig into two graham-cracker-and-chocolate sandwiches. "Are you ready for this?"

Bobby nodded, and Slimey passed him a s'more. They bit down at the same time. Bobby's eyes widened as he chewed. "Whoa! This is the best thing I've ever tasted!"

"Told you."

"My mom would never let me eat this at home."

"Lucky for you, you have one more day to do whatever you would never be allowed to do at home."

Half a day, Bobby thought. It had been seven weeks plus three days so far, and being here with Slimey and the San Juan Hillers, he wished there were more.

"You ready, buddy?" Rick asked him, motioning to a bit of marshmallow stuck above Bobby's lip.

More than I've ever been, Bobby thought. "Yup." He wiped his mouth with the sleeve of his hoodie and pushed himself up from the log.

"Ready for what?" Slimey asked.

"You'll see," he said, arching an eyebrow. He walked with Rick around the campfire. Rick handed him his guitar.

"You're gonna rock it, buddy."

"As long as I don't pull a Campstock and panic," he joked. Campstock felt like forever ago, and although Bobby was sure he'd have plenty of panic attacks in the future, there was no way Bizarro was getting the best of him now. Rick put his fist out for a pound. Bobby pounded him back, and Rick dipped under Bobby's fist with a peace sign.

"Snail!" they said together. It was go time.

"All right, everybody. Smell—I mean, Bobby, here—"

"It's OK. You can call me Smelly. I kind of like it."

"Awesome! Smelly, here," Rick continued, "is going to perform a little something he's been working on. Let's give it up for SMELLY!"

Everyone clapped with the same enthusiasm they'd welcomed him with that very first day. This time, though, it didn't freak him out. It made him feel great. He pulled Rick's strap over his shoulder, strummed a G chord, then launched into the chord progression Rick had taught him. He sang the lyrics he'd written during the first couple weeks of camp. He couldn't stop thinking about Slimey then, and it was no different now.

"I'm in a kerfuffle, 'cause even on shuffle
I can't get you out of my mind.
If it's rock, rap, or reggae, don't matter what I play,
You're in every lyric I find.
I've got twenty gigs of memories,
And all of them are you.
All the songs on my iPod make me think of you."

By the time he finished, everyone was standing, whooping, and cheering. Bobby saw Slimey glowing across the campfire. He felt like Superman.

"Hey, Smelly! Where's *my* love song?" Play Dough joked.

"Wiener didn't sing it to you yet?" Bobby joked back. "Oh, shoot, I spoiled your Valentine's Day surprise."

"Ohhhh!" The San Juaners and Anita Hillers laughed.

Bobby lifted Rick's guitar strap over his head and walked back to Slimey. Missi caught his arm on the way. "You're a rhythm prodigy. We should do a flute-guitar duet sometime."

"Thanks! That sounds . . ."

"Amazing, I know. You don't have to say it."

Totle jumped in. "Discovery consists of seeing what everybody has seen but thinking what nobody has thought."

"What about me?" Sophie asked. "Can you, like, discover something about me?"

Totle stared into Sophie's eyes and gently moved her long bangs from her face. "You have a bug bite on your forehead." Sophie sighed dramatically.

Bobby took a seat next to Slimey on the log.

"I have chills from that song," she whispered, beaming.

He smiled back. "Maybe next summer I'll actually sing it at Campstock."

"Next summer? What about baseball camp?"

"Well, I was thinking of trying out for my school team instead. They're supposed to be really good, and I bet I could be pitcher if I practice hard. I'm gonna ask my mom and dad to sign me up for guitar lessons, too. That way, when I come back, I can jam with Rick, kind of like a band."

He felt Slimey's hand glide into his. "Bobby, remember how I told you: sometimes it hits you when you're home at the end of the summer, and you're, like—?"

"Wow, that was amazing. I'm reverse homesick. I'm campsick?"

"Looks like you're ahead of the game."

When Slimey had told him that during their first coed Evening Activity, never in a million years did he think he'd miss this place. But she was right. Here he was, feeling as sentimental and mushy as all his friends, who he'd once thought were weird and part of a freakish cult. Well, he still wasn't sure about the cult part.

Rick put his arm around Sara. This time, she didn't push him away. "All right, everyone, roast your last marshmallow. It's getting late."

"I can't believe it's over already," Melman said, resting her elbow on Slimey's left shoulder. "My flight to London's tomorrow, and school's in, like, T-minus eighteen days. Blech."

"I know—blech," Steinberg repeated.

"Oh, please. You love school," Melman said.

"First of all, *love*'s a strong word. I *like* science at school, but I *love* science at camp, where there's no adult supervision."

"That's a good one, Steinberg," Rick said. "Now shove that s'more into your mouth and say good-bye." He and Sara stood up.

"Booooooo!" the campers all moaned, throwing their sticks into the fire. They watched the flames grow larger and larger.

"Hey, hey . . . enough with the negativity," Rick said. "You'll all be back. And if you miss this place, all you have to do is think about the fun you had, the friends you've made, and you'll warm yourself up even on the coldest winter day."

"You are such a sap!" Sara laughed.

After a long hug session with the teary-eyed Anita Hillers, the boys and girls got ready to go their separate ways. Bobby looked at Slimey, her dark brown eyes shimmering like they had at the dance. He could feel himself getting choked up, trying to voice a good-bye that let her know how lucky he felt to be with her, and how he'd miss her, and that he hoped to see her soon, since they only lived two towns over, and his mom could drive them to the movies, or his dad to a baseball game—but she stopped him.

"Don't do it. You and me, we have a three-hour ride to say good-bye tomorrow. Save me a seat if you get on first!" Slimey left Bobby with a peck on the cheek and an ear-to-ear smile.

Bobby grinned, because she was right. They might have been at the end of day fifty-two, but the summer wasn't over yet.

Ten Months for Two

Slimey and Bobby sat eighteen rows back in the bus destined for the Paramus Park Mall. They each had one of Slimey's earbuds in, listening to "Blackbird" on Bobby's dad's iPod. With Boy from the Bus as her bus buddy and boyfriend, Slimey found the ride home way better than the ride to camp had been.

The song ended, and Bobby looked at Slimey with a determined smile. "OK, we've got about fifteen minutes left. Should we do this?"

"Yup!" Slimey dug into her purple L.L.Bean backpack and took out her sketchpad. She flipped to page twenty-four, where she'd once drawn Bobby's brown L.L.Bean backpack and had since sketched in how she remembered him from that first day. Red shorts, blue shirt, gray sweatshirt, hard-core headphones, warm brown eyes, tousled hair—crazy cute. Slimey carefully tore it out and folded it in half.

Bobby was waiting for her, paper bag in hand. "Who should go first? Or should we exchange at the same time?"

"Well, I don't want you to look at the sketch until you're home, in bed, about to go to sleep. And just remember that art is impressionistic, and don't get a nose job."

"I'll be sure not to . . . change my nose," Bobby said with a smirk. "So, then, do you want to save mine, too?"

"No way! I'm too excited. And impatient. And excited." She giggled.

"OK, then. Here you go. I made it in Arts and Crafts with Melman's help." Bobby handed her the paper bag, and she opened it to find an oversize hemp necklace.

Hanging from the center was a large wooden locket, the size and shape of a heart. Inside was a bunch of camp paraphernalia: their Canteen Cards, a list of their favorite songs, and cut-up photographs of her and the Anita Hill girls. As Slimey looked through it, she could feel her smile growing wider and wider, her cheeks getting hot. This even beat the old pair of Slimey's jean shorts that her mom had sewn into a pillow for everyone in her cabin to sign, and the hilarious "Last Will and Testament" Sara wrote each summer based on their cabin's inside jokes. "This is the nicest thing anyone's ever done for me."

Bobby grinned back at her. "To make up for the one I took. It might be something cool to hang on your wall or off your bedpost."

"Definitely. And you can hang yours, too, if you want, but I think it would be cool if you carried it with you. Like, in your backpack or something, so, in a way, I'm always close."

"Done." Bobby stuck his pinky out, and they shook. He'd gotten good at camp-speak.

"So, who's picking you up? Mom or Dad?"

"Both, actually. They're still getting a divorce, but they've agreed to meet me together."

"That's really nice."

"My dad said he'd bring me French toast to eat in the car, and my mom promised not to freak out if powdered sugar gets on the leather seats of her Honda."

"Wow, homemade French toast sounds sooo good right now."

"Oh! I meant to ask. So, what's the deal with the moon thing at ten o'clock? Are we supposed to just break out into song in our backyards?"

"Yup! It's like a good-night, good-bye sort of thing."

"Cool. Well . . . maybe if you want, after tonight, we can say—not sing—good night to each other at the moon. You know how much I love singing in public, but I don't want to get any neighborhood noise complaints."

Slimey giggled. "Done."

They pinky-swore again.

She plugged the earbuds into her iPod shuffle, which was filled with pop and techno and indie music from this decade, not the 1960s. It was her turn. Bobby leaned against the window with his knees a little bit bent, the tips of his Nikes against the back of the seat in front of them. Slimey rested her head on his shoulder and felt his hand take hers.

Too soon, the bus rolled into the Paramus Park Mall parking lot, which was filled with cheering parents. Slimey peered through the window and spotted her mom blowing air kisses at her. Her heart swelled with excitement, until she looked back at Bobby and was reminded that she was about to leave him and the best summer of her life behind. She slipped Bobby's locket around her neck alongside the one from her dad. "I know we'll see each other, but remember to sing, or say, good night to the moon."

"Every day until next summer," he said with a smile. "A whole forty-four weeks plus four and a half days."

Bobby was right. She'd done the math last night, too.

The countdown started now.

Sophster (ha-ha, we should actually call u that!),

This summer has been amazing. OMG, you are so weird, but we love you, and we'd be, like, nothing without you. The ransom note you wrote to the boys was insane.

LOVE, KISSES, HUGS,
The J-Squad (Jenny wrote this—Jamie is next to me for support)

Whassup Slimes,

I hope you like the "surprise" I put together with your not-so-smelly, not-so-bad BF. He's sweet, just like you. I'm gonna miss your face, like, whoa, but can't wait to Skype you first thing in the morning my time and the middle of the night your time. Your mom will love that.

Love you more than camp itself,
Melman

Yo, P.D. . . . bet's still on. If I get two armpit hairs by next summer, you owe me ten bucks and a dirty mag.

—Wiener

Hey, P.D:
As promised, you get the raid map. Now frame it.
—Dover

Hi Jenny!
This summer was amazing. I'll never forget when you had the idea to steal the boys' underwear. So funny. Also, you are so pretty. I know I tell you that, like, every day, but it's true. You and Jamie should be models.
MEOOOOW,
Missi

Hi Jenny,

Have a good summer WiNTeR.
You're cool.

Play Dough

Hello Jamie,
I know sometimes I told you vampire stories and you got nightmares, but I think that means you're destined to love them. Here is a recommended BOOK list:
Howling at the Sun Part I
Howling at the Sun Part II
Howling at the Sun Part III
Vampires Suck
Vampira the Vamp
Pale as Death
I can ship them to you from Florida, or you can read them on a Kindle if you have one. (I've never seen you read.)
Sophie

Mel,
What can I say? This summer went by in a flash. I love you so much, and I am so lucky to have you. Be prepared to Skype A LOT. Next summer in faith Hill Cabin is gonna be the best summer yet (hard to believe cause this summer was SOOOO AMAZING!).
Your soul sis & BFFAEAE,
Slimey

Miss Missi,

I'm gonna miss ur funniness and ur cat poster. (That is not an invitation to send me Buttercup Whiskers III's hairball like u did last year, but I guess he's dead, so I'm safe). Ur funny so much.

XO,
Jamieeeeee

Hey Steinberg,
Thanks for everything. Vaseline helps wedgies, by the way. Can't wait for next summer at the Hills!
Smelly

Dover, here's how you make a robot:
www.howtomakearobothesteinbergway.com
From,
Steinberg

Smelly,

"There is nothing better than a friend, unless it is a friend who has rescued our underwear."

—Totle

Acknowledgments

A few years ago, I was lucky to collaborate with the Spiegel brothers—Adam and David—on writing the musical *Camp Rolling Hills*. My friend Erica Finkel saw a workshop of the show and tossed out the idea that I write a book for middle schoolers. A few months later, I embarked on *Camp Rolling Hills:* the book! Erica is my fairy godmother, bestie, and editor, who grew the seed of an idea into a full-fledged series. I am forever grateful. Thank you to the amazing Spiegel brothers for your inspiration and permission to nurture the world we hold so close to our hearts.

Camp has been a major part of my life and still is. I was lucky to transition from camper to counselor to upper staff at Tyler Hill Camp, where my mom was the Head of Girls' Side. Mom and Dad, thank you for introducing me to this incredible, life-changing place, for daring me to be silly and take enormous risks, and for your endless love and support. To my brother, Mike, my sister, Amy, and my sister-in-law, Deanna, who all work in the camp industry: congrats on making a career out of the greatest cult. I love you.

Grandma Terry, Grandma Joanie, and Grandpa Lenny, thank you for being my number one fans. You three are the world's best.

Lauren Kasnett Nearpass, thank you for brainstorming marketing and branding and for inviting me to blog for Summer 365. I'm honored to be working with you and your incredible organization.

Aimee Berger, you're a rock star. Thanks to you, It's a Camp Thing, and Camplified for all your summer coordination and support!

Jay Jacobs, thank you for conceiving the STARFISH Program and for granting me permission to reference it in the Camp Rolling Hills series. It's a brilliant values system that defined so much of my personal experience at Tyler Hill. I'm so glad I can share it.

Lexi Korologos, my teenage life coach, thank you for reading countless drafts, dishing your honest feedback, and brainstorming titles.

Susan Van Metre, Erica Finkel (again and again), and the whole brilliant team at Abrams: Pam, Jim, Jen, Michael, Jason, Caitlin, Jess, Mary, Elisa, Rob, and Kathy. Thank you for seeing so much potential in an early draft and for providing the feedback that has enriched the story a million times over.

Thank you to my friend and collaborator Elissa Brent Weissman for introducing me to my agent, Erica Rand Silverman. Erica, I'm so lucky to have such a camp-loving, fierce advocate of my work.

My camp friends. My campers. My counselors. My co-counselors. The camps: Twin Oaks, Crestwood, Summit, Tyler Hill, A.C.T., Oxbridge. You have made me who I am today and provided me with the heart and experience to write this series.

My partner-in-crime, Tim Borecky, thank you for lending me your wisdom and dramaturgy every time I cornered you to read you chapters. I appreciate your indulging my characters as if they are our friends.

To all the camp people out there, enjoy the adventure and the s'mores.

About the Author

Stacy Davidowitz is a camp-obsessed writer of books, plays, and screenplays. She also enjoys acting, singing, running long distances, and teaching theater all over New York City. Her alma maters are Tufts University, Columbia University, and Tyler Hill Camp. The Camp Rolling Hills series marks her debut as an author. Visit Stacy at www.stacydavidowitz.com and www.camprollinghills.com

Head back to the Hills in Book Two: Crossing Over.

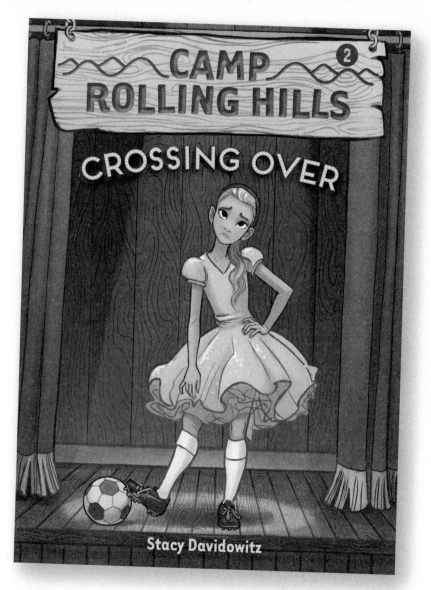

Available now!